Wild Prep

Wild Prep

Crazy Beautiful Life

Alex Gonzalez

authorHOUSE®

AuthorHouse™
1663 Liberty Drive
Bloomington, IN 47403
www.authorhouse.com
Phone: 1-800-839-8640

First published by AuthorHouse   12/20/2011

ISBN: 978-1-4685-2425-3 (sc)
ISBN: 978-1-4685-2424-6 (hc)
ISBN: 978-1-4685-2423-9 (ebk)

Library of Congress Control Number: 2011962044

Printed in the United States of America

This book is dedicated to Becky Kalma.

"I'm in love, alright with my crazy beautiful life. With the parties, the disasters with my friends all pretty and plastered."

Ke$ha—"Crazy Beautiful Life"

Acknowledgments

Wow, I can't believe I'm actually writing one of these. First off, I would like to thank my mom, who was so supportive when I told her about my decision to invest in the publication of my writing. I would also like to thank my younger brother, who helped me do the things that I really didn't want to do, such as reading the manuscript over and over, and gave me advice on how to improve. Becky Kalma was the most amazing person in making *Wild Prep* the best it could be. Thank you so much for investing the time (two very long, stressful, but fun years), editing, and giving me your input, not just on *Wild Prep* but also on all my other pieces of writing. Without you, my writing would not be nearly as good as it could be. I would like to thank Sandy Nordyke, who also took time from her schedule to edit and round off some of the jagged corners of *Wild Prep*. Last but not least, I would like to thank my AuthorHouse team—Leandro McMont, who got in contact with me two years after my initial response. My check-in coordinator, Margaret Michna, helped me step by step, and also thanks to my marketing consultant, Jason Beck. Thank you all for helping make my dream come true!

Introduction

Welcome to *Miami Teen Social*, a magazine/website that offers a defined look at Miami's privileged young people. Here at *MTS*, we give Average Joes like you a peep inside the shameful lives of students who attend Hamilton Prep, and other surrounding exclusive prep schools. We cover unabashed heiresses and their wild male counterparts (heirs), offspring of the rich and unknown, and cultured yet secretive socialites. And then from time to time we get our fair share of actual DNA spawn from bona fide celebrities and professional athletes. We report what our insiders tell us, backed up with proof. Our "paps" capture nothing but raw images of these creatures out and about. It may seem like an out-of-this-world life: continuous parties, never-ending bank accounts, and looks that would make any plastic surgeon envious. But it's these kids' lives, and they are truly Wild Preps.

Ahh, so it seems that summer vacation is over for the Hamilton Prep students in Miami, Florida. Parties are over, posh vacations are out, and school is back in session. For the new class, it is freshman year, and with that brings new relationships, new discoveries, new drama, and, of course, less importantly, new grueling classes.

The new "fresh meat" of Hamilton Prep have decided to start things off with a bonfire by the beach right after their orientation. Their chauffeur-driven Mercedes, BMWs, Jaguars, Bentleys, and Range Rovers are parked to the side. Their gated mansions or beachside condos are being cleaned by maids, and their well-to-do parents, of course, are doing their thing, being absent as always. Good thing those parents left "trusted" chaperones in charge of the preps. Like the parents, those chaperones oversee the preps; like the preps, those chaperones are wild! Let's get to know this new class, which seems all too wonderful.

First, there's Lily Carrington, class president and daughter of Senator Carrington. She enjoys reading, riding, and watching the news. Unbeknownst to everyone else, the senator threatened to deprive her of her trust fund if she didn't win the class vote for the presidency. It appears that everything is not perfect at the Carrington house. For some time now, Lily has had a major crush on Talan Merrick, the eye-catching jock and son of former famed Miami Dolphins receiver Donald Merrick. Not known to many, Lily's biggest problem is knowing who her friends are, and more important, knowing if she even has any.

Talan Merrick voted for Lily for president, only because he wasn't even paying attention to the class elections and just picked the first name his brain managed to focus on. Although he is, by far, the best freshman athlete, few people know that his father paid coaches early on to play his son more, and sent Talan to exhausting football camps starting at age twelve. To his friends, Talan was simply at his mom's at the time. Talan enjoys sports, trying to get with girls, and sports. This summer, Talan got to stay in Miami, and it was in this time that he developed a fling with Sasha Chandler, the daughter of a small-time fashion model whose career ended when she got pregnant. Luckily for her, three years later she married a CFO of a major *Fortune* Five Hundred company. Also, unrevealed to many, Talan has always struggled with image, but why would an attractive, wealthy, fit young man feel that way—maybe his father has a teeny part in it.

Sasha Chandler has never even thought about struggling with her self-image. Her mother is indeed a former fashion model. One look at Sasha, and one immediately thinks, *Bitch*. Think again—behind the exterior of this perfect teenager is actually a young girl who wishes everyone could be attractive and nice. At age nine, she was taking her allowance and donating one-third of it to her Catholic church. What is her imperfection, which is unknown to everyone? Sasha has dated a lot of people, but none that she was ever serious about. She couldn't fall in love when she was preoccupied with an underlying secret. Talan Merrick is the first guy she has seen as a potential boyfriend candidate. Let's just see how things pan out between the two this year.

Johnson Sinclair is an heir to the major Sinclair family fortune. Of course, all Florida residents, especially Miami residents, know that the Sinclairs' money fuels Miami. Johnson is a major-label whore, and he doesn't care how much Calvin Klein or Armani costs to fly all the way from New York to Miami, as long as he has it by that night. Johnson, of course, is gay. Johnson loves to go clubbing. The social magazines have all reported on his wild partying, along with Talan's, and they also have reported on his major spending, along with Sasha's. It seems that Johnson may have it all—money, friends, power, and money; however, he hasn't spoken to his father in years. Not for the obvious reasons—his father is actually in hiding overseas. To everyone else, his father is doing business, but what father would be doing business for two years overseas?

Of course there are so, so many more students in Hamilton Prep's new freshman class, but with these four, why bother reporting on them? This is *Miami Teen Social*. Thanks for reading. Until next time . . .

Chapter One

First Day of Class

The bonfire weekend is over, and it's the first official day of high school for these spoiled brats. They trudge into school, hungover and already tired, while their teachers are overwhelmed by having students with such controversial relatives in their classrooms. Why don't we take a good look at the first day of school?

"Mr. Berndt, I really think that the freshman lockers need to be relocated. For me, it's a hassle going all the way to B wing, and then back to my journalism class," Lily stated, already campaigning and using her power as the new freshman class president. Poor Lily was already getting petitions ready.

"Miss Carrington, I really think it's not possible for that to happen," Mr. Berndt replied, scared of hurting the senator's daughter's feelings.

"But Mr. Berndt!" Lily complained, swinging her metallic Marc Jacobs bag. Even though Lily was a bookworm and had virtually no friends, she loved her fashion. In addition to disliking that her journalism class was so far, she detested the uniforms at Hamilton Prep. As an alternative to the standard bulky clogs she had to wear, Lily had swapped them for some fab white Stuart Weitzman heels.

"God, Lily is already complaining about something," Johnson told Sasha as they stood next to their lockers eyeing everyone walking by.

"I know, right? But do you think if we asked Lily to hang out with us, maybe she wouldn't be so annoying?" Sasha suggested. Sasha Chandler also had made some modifications to her uniform. She had hiked her skirt up, unbuttoned a couple of the buttons on her shirt to show off a little extra, and had long black tights with some Manolo Blahniks in place of the clogs.

"Ugh, I'm not going to spend my time with Lily Carrington. Her voice is annoying enough, and I don't want to be looking at her face all day."

"That's not very nice, Johnson."

"No, not nice is having my chinchilla's fur falling out 'cause she broke her leg, and having the stupid vet load her up with the wrong medicine, and then giving her more medicine to try to fix the problem," he said while checking his phone for messages. Sasha looked behind him to see Talan walking steadily over toward them. She almost lost her breath as she saw him looking so dashing in the standard Hamilton Prep uniform, which consisted of a white shirt, tie, slacks, and dark blue blazer.

"Hey, Talan," she said, smiling cutely.

"Hey, Sasha. What's up, Johnson?" Talan replied, just so suave.

"Nothing much-hungover and bitchy," Johnson said back.

"And when are you not?" Sasha chimed in.

"This was fun, but I'm totally out. The new bio teacher is hot, and I want to get a tardy so I can stay after school. 'Bye, freaks." Johnson grabbed his books and headed out.

"'Bye," Sasha and Talan both said.

"So, how do you like high school so far?" Talan asked Sasha, not knowing where to start the conversation. Talan almost never had a problem breaking the ice, but with Sasha it was different. He really wanted things to work out with her. She was the first girl who gave him chills—how cute. Talan could have any girl he wanted. Sasha—could she handle the pressure of being with such a noted Merrick family member?

"It's going fine. Johnson and I don't have many classes together, which I guess is a good thing," she said, smiling and trying to sound humorous. Talan smiled at seeing her adorable smile.

"Tonight there is this opening. It's this cool, chill place downtown in South Beach, and I was wondering if you wanted to go with me?" Talan asked, anxious about what her answer would be.

"Yeah, I would love to," she answered.

"Cool." Talan came in to hug her, but Sasha suddenly flinched. "Oh, sorry."

"No, no, it's okay. I'm sorry. I should get to class." Sasha quickly got her books and walked to class, mortified.

As the day went on, the kids found themselves drained and already standing by to go home. Lunch break provided an escape. Lunch at Hamilton Prep is like any other lunch at any other school. The cafeteria is still full of cliques, even though everyone has trusts and butlers. Okay, so tables are broken into hobbies. Hobbies are broken into appearance. Appearance displays power and popularity. The popular jocks, such as Talan Merrick and his go-to guy, Faiday Hayward, all sit together. Pretty girls, such as Sasha Chandler, all sit together along with people like Johnson Sinclair. Tables are still filled with nerds and goths/atheists, and there are even overachievers, who are very different from the nerds. Lily Carrington finds herself at that table. She has an apple and a banana beside her, but she is too busy telling people to sign her petition for switching lockers.

"Do you ever wonder what it would be like to sit at that table?" Sasha asked Johnson, while she was looking over at Talan's table. Talan noticed her looking over and smiled. Sasha, still embarrassed by their encounter earlier, shyly smiled back.

"No," Johnson replied blandly. "I do, however, wonder why they make us wear uniforms when it's so hot," he said as he took off his blazer. Soon Sasha's phone buzzed—with a text from Talan.

There's room over here, if u want to sit wit us

Sasha managed to crack a silly smile. She's known Talan for quite a while, but in Miami, it's hard to get one-on-one time with someone unless you make room for it.

Okay ☺

"Emily, let's sit with Talan, and them." Sasha got up, bringing one of her friends.

"Okay," Emily replied, just too happy. As Sasha walked over and sat with Talan, Johnson quickly took over the conversation at the table. Looks like a certain someone is ready for the queen bee to be exiled and a king bee to emerge.

"Hey," Talan replied as Sasha and Emily sat down. "Excited for tonight?"

"Definitely," Sasha said. For the next twenty minutes Sasha and Talan talked about the sun and the moon—while Johnson told all the girls and Sasha's little followers about his expensive vacation to Fiji that he took over the summer.

The universe has to watch over a new romance that is certainly blossoming, and a new leader who might materialize, but in the land of Hamilton Prep things are up one day and down the next. Signing off for the first day of class, it's *Miami Teen Social,* until tonight, when drama will surely erupt.

Chapter Two

New Openings and Surprises

It's 9:30, the warm breeze is out, disco balls are in, and it's time to play. The first day was exhausting for the pitiable students of Hamilton Prep, but that's not stopping them from having a wild night out on the town.

"Where did you say you were going out tonight?" Johnson asked Sasha as she straightened her long blond hair. Sasha and Johnson were at Sasha's place, a calming Zen-inspired home in beautiful Coral Gables. Johnson liked to go over to Sasha's just to see if there was a family more messed up than his. What a great friend.

"It's this club place down at South Beach," Sasha replied. Oh, and it looks as if once again that Mommy and dead Daddy's money are letting these unruly children break the rules by entering a club when they are clearly underage. "Do you want to come?"

"No, thanks. I have better things to do than see you and Talan throwing yourselves at each other." Johnson laughed. "A couple of the girls and I are going to Peek-A-Boo, and seeing what we find," Johnson went on while rolling his eyes, already anticipating the night.

"Well, don't drink too much," Sasha warned, knowing about Johnson's wild party lifestyle.

"You know I will."

Talan decided to pick Sasha up in, of course, a limo. Sasha dressed in a gold sparkly Burberry mini that cost approximately $4,500. With Step-Daddy gone, Sasha and her mother received a bulky life insurance check, along with all his properties.

"You look incredible," Talan said, almost going in for a hug, but stopping once he remembered what had happened at school. Talan is a real romantic, but behind all that is a major douche, a future womanizer.

"Thanks, and so do you," Sasha replied, with butterflies in her stomach. Talan was dressed in a dark red Calvin Klein button-up and some black slacks. Talan looked up behind her at the glass doors leading into her stylish-looking house to see a woman standing scandalously in a bra and underwear with only a loose robe covering her from the warm Miami breeze—it seems that Lenny, Sasha's mom, had a little too much to drink.

"Mom!" Sasha said in a sharp, embarrassed tone.

"Well, who is this, but Talan Merrick?" Lenny walked down. "Son of Don Merrick. Why, Sasha, you didn't tell me you were dating him." Her words clung together.

"Mom, we're not dating." Sasha looked down self-consciously at how her mom was revealing everything, which she had worked hard to cover.

"It's nice to meet you, Mrs. Chandler," Talan greeted her, trying to make the situation less awkward.

"Please, Lenny," Ms. Chandler replied. "I want you home no later than one; it's a school night."

"Yes, Mom," Sasha responded as she quickly got into the limo with Talan. Someone will have to explain why her mother is such a sloppy drunk.

"I'm sorry about her. Ever since my stepfather died, she has just fallen off the deep end," Sasha explained, trying to play it modest.

"It's okay. I understand," Talan soothed Sasha, trying to act as if his family were perfect.

Once Talan and Sasha arrived at the opening of the new nightclub in South Beach, they entered in the back way. Music welcomed the duo as they enter the neon-lighted club.

"Thanks for bringing me here," Sasha said, smiling. She quickly got closer to the warmth of Talan, and started to move with the flow of the music. Talan nuzzled his soft nose against Sasha's elongated neck. She giggled with pleasure The pair soon started to dance and enjoy themselves.

After they were dancing awhile, Talan ordered a couple drinks (hoping he'd get lucky. Then again, Merricks never needed luck) and handed one to Sasha. Sasha daintily took a sip and, not liking the taste of alcohol, set it down. When she looked back up, Talan had his half gone. Talan smirked charmingly and grabbed her hand. They went back out onto the dance floor, where they danced—if you want to call it that—a little vulgarly. They were on the dance floor for the next couple of hours, dancing like it was their last night on earth. If only that were true.

"I'm really glad you came," Talan told Sasha while they were taking a break from dancing. They were sitting down in one of the booths, enjoying talking to each other.

"Thanks, and so am I." Talan could barely hear her over the thud of the music. They looked up to see that Faiday Hayward, one of Talan's best friends and an all-around jock, was with Emily Parker, one of Sasha's best friends, and an all-around bitch. Faiday and Emily were almost the Avril and Deryck of the group. Faiday had a hint of bad boy with his don't care approach to everything. He cussed like a sailor, and also had a splash of punk in him. He always wore his tie loosely around his neck (which would drive Headmaster Trimble up the wall), and he would never tuck in his shirt, yet all that was wrapped into a jock label. He liked football and was good at it. Emily Parker was into fashion labels and dressing up like she was some socialite, but despite wearing Gucci and Prada, she, too, was a bit of a rebel.

"You came!" Sasha cheered as she hugged her Emily. The four sat and chatted awhile, getting their pictures taken by photographers—the young socials of Miami out on the town.

"Sasha, I really want to see how things work out with us, and how far we can take this," Talan said seriously as he whispered into Sasha's ear, while holding her hands and dancing. Sasha had a hard time believing him, knowing he had drank quite a bit, but she convinced herself that they were meant to be together. How young teenage love works these days is so immature and brainless. Let's just hope cute little Sasha doesn't get hurt—that badly.

"I do too." Sasha played with Talan's tousled blond hair and looked deep inside his gorgeous blue eyes. She realized he was the hottest boy she'd ever seen. She thought that it was too much of a moment to pass up, so their lips touched for fifteen seconds—it would have lasted longer, but it was already close to one. "I have to go," Sasha said, frowning unhappily. Now Sasha isn't one for breaking rules. Even though she knew her mom was probably not home, she wanted to be home on time.

"See you tomorrow." Talan kissed her once again before she departed. Talan looked around for Faiday once Sasha had left, but as he walked back to the booth, he saw only Emily. Wonder what will happen?

Meanwhile, at Peek-A-Boo, a local nightclub, Johnson was partying away, having way too much fun for a fifteen-year-old. Once again, his mother had to go to Paris for some business, taking his little sister with her and leaving Johnson in the company of the maids and his worthless chaperone. Johnson had had too much to drink, and after dancing with some random person who bored him, he walked back up to his booth, only to discover some frienemies had taken refuge there.

"What the hell is this?" Johnson asked, with a huge headache from all of the Cosmos he had just consumed.

"Umm, we're sitting here," Lizzy Van Ryan pointed out. Lizzy Van Ryan attended the holy Miami Catholic Prep school. Yes, Miami *Catholic* Prep, which is a huge rival to Hamilton. There's nothing Jesus loves more than to see His children drinking at nightclubs and acting like fools.

"Why don't you say a little prayer to your priest, and get the hell out, 'cause I, like, own this place," Johnson informed her as he grabbed a drink from a passing waiter and took a mouthful.

"Johnson, you don't own anything in South Beach!" Lizzy shouted, clearly annoyed by his presence.

"My family runs Miami. Your family is just some wannabe Hamilton Prep rejects! My pet chinchilla can get into Miami Catholic Prep school! You're so pathetic," Johnson shouted at the top of his lungs. Lizzy then calmly exchanged some rumors that she had heard about him, and it basically ended with Johnson throwing his drink. Johnson heard a scream and quickly exited the club. One rule of being a social is to always have a quick way out when you need one. Johnson did just that, exiting into his Mercedes and having his driver peel off into the heavy Miami traffic.

It looks like we've got some juicy topics for the next issue. We captured dirty dancing between a former footballer's son and a former model's daughter. Then we got what Talan Merrick did or didn't do when Sasha left. Could this really be the girl for him? Well, who is to say that high school romances won't last? Then, of course, we got Johnson Sinclair acting out—once again. Can this famous heir ever get it together? Signing off once again, it's *Miami Teen Social.*

Chapter Three

Tabloids

One condition of being a teen social in Miami is to make an appearance in the tabloids. Don't think that we're desperate and pathetic by reporting on wild, privileged teens who need serious reality checks. It's a recession out here, and we do what we have to in order to survive. We don't all have deep pockets like the Sinclairs. Tabloids work fast and can get news out there in a matter of hours—but one thing is certain, many people always say to never believe everything you read, but with *Miami Teen Social* we make sure that our pictures are worth a thousand *true* words . . .

"I'm so hungover," Johnson made known to Sasha as they sat in the lounge at Hamilton Prep together. Today Johnson decided to show up in sunglasses, to hide his bloodshot eyes, his messy hair, and his terrible attitude. Sasha, however, showed no signs that she was out past midnight. Some girls can roll out of bed and look like they just jumped off the runway, and Sasha was one of them.

"God, what did you do last night?" she asked as she took a drink of her low-fat cappuccino.

"Went to Peek-A-Boo, where Frizzy Lizzy took my booth, that whore," he whined as he leaned his shoulder against Sasha, ready to fall back asleep.

"I kissed Talan last night." Sasha smiled, informing her best friend.

"Eww."

"Don't act like you wouldn't," she said, laughing. As she and Johnson continued their conversation, Lily was heading to class. Unlike the rest of her classmates, Lily had been in bed by ten thirty. She stayed up late working on an English essay.

"Mrs. Mulberry, I have that essay you told us to do for English about what we spent the summer doing to conserve energy and go green," she advised as she handed her English teacher her assignment.

"Oh, Miss Carrington, that's not due until the end of the week." Mrs. Mulberry was surprised that a student would have finished it already. That was Lily for you.

"I had time last night, and I printed it on recycled paper, too," Lily informed her.

"Miss Carrington, you're going to make an amazing student this year. Your father must be so proud." Ouch—big mistake, Nancy Mulberry. Playing the father card on Lily Carrington will get you no favors. Her father is such a sensitive subject for her—how clever. This gives the magazine some ideas now. Lily forced a smile and went to her desk in the front row. Lily, by all standards, is an attractive girl. She's one of those people who seem so cool when you look at her, but once she opens her mouth it's just a big old disarray of annoyingness—but isn't it that way with any Hamilton Prep student? Lily has long, dark auburn hair; it falls slightly below her elbows. She has these piercing round brown eyes, and dark bangs right above them. She missed out on the Miami gene, and doesn't enjoy going to the beach much; consequently, her skin is an unattractive pale color.

Once it got to third hour, it appeared that Johnson's day had gotten a little better. That is, until one of his "friends" approached him with some news, which he didn't want to hear.

"Oh, my God, Johnson! You're on *Miami Teen Social*," Hannah Reynolds, whom Johnson utterly hated, told him.

"What? Again?" Johnson replied, without a doubt annoyed by the article we wrote on him.

"Yeah, I just read it."

"What did it say?" Johnson asked, alarmed.

"Come on, Johnson. It's the second day of school. You can waste my time some other day," Señor Carlos said as he tried to usher Johnson into Spanish class. Some people loathed the Sinclair family for several different reasons. Señor Carlos, one of the Hamilton Prep Spanish teachers, was one of them. *Miami Teen Social* loves Johnson. We really do, but it's for work-related purposes. With an article on him, our magazine gets loads of views. As soon as Señor Carlos closed the door and walked up to front of the classroom, Johnson popped out his phone and quickly logged on to our website. Sure enough, he read the article.

> It seems that while Mommy and Daddy are gone, heir and all-around party boy Johnson Sinclair will . . . throw drinks? Yes, it is true, Johnson finally stooped to drink-slinging last night at Peek-A-Boo. We all knew it would eventually come to that. After partying it away, at around one thirty in the morning, he discovered rival and one-time friend Lizzy Van Ryan sitting in his usual booth. It appeared that he didn't have any cash folds to throw, but only his drink. After a heated argument between the pair, he, in fact, threw the drink, striking poor Frizzy Lizzy across the head. Police were called, but by then Johnson was long gone. It looks as if Frizzy Lizzy will be pressing charges against the famous Miami heir. Let's see how much it will cost to get him out of this.

"Oh, my God, charges?" Johnson swore. It seemed that this was a situation Johnson didn't think he would be able to get out of like the rest. However, Johnson wasn't the only one making headlines in *Miami Teen Social*.

At cheerleading practice, the same hour, Sasha was having a fun time with the girls telling them all how much fun she had last night with Talan and what a perfect guy he was.

"He's so nice and polite. He's not like the rest of the guys I've dated," Sasha said giddily.

"How sweet, and it doesn't hurt that he is the hottest boy in school either," Jennifer pointed out as Sasha's little group of popular girls lay down on the football field, taking a break from the exhausting cheerleading warm-ups of jumping jacks and girls' push-ups. Sasha smiled, realizing it was true.

"Did you hear about Johnson?" Lorraine Everly, one of Johnson and Sasha's best friends, asked as she finishing reading the article about him in *Miami Teen Social*. Just as she was about to hand Sasha her phone, she scrolled down a little, and saw another article.

"Oh, my God," Lorraine gasped as she read the article aloud.

> The statement, "like father, like son" seems to be accurately true here. Last night, Talan Merrick, son of famous playboy and Dolphins receiver Don Merrick, celebrated the opening of Chic, a new nightclub down at South Beach, by snuggling up against Sasha Chandler and some friends (Pictured to the left, Faiday Hayward, Emily Parker, Sasha Chandler, and Talan Merrick, all sitting down). The two danced very risqué, almost to the point that you would think Sasha would have been impregnated, or maybe they were celebrating their first day of *high school*. The two were also reportedly making out like wild apes during mating season. Then after Sasha left in the wee hours, Talan was pictured nuzzling up against Emily Parker, daughter of Galvin Parker of Sonnet Enterprises, who showed up with Talan's close friend. Wonder how Sasha will take this thing.

Sasha's innocent eyes welled up with tears. Oh, how sweet betrayal feels when you're fifteen. You just feel like it's the end of the world.

"Oh, I'm sorry, Sasha," Jennifer said, feeling just as sad as her leader.

"Me, too," Lorraine eased in, with a hint of a wicked smile. While the girls comforted Sasha, Talan was being praised for his victory in "conquering" two girls in one night.

"I knew it." Ashton Cross grinned arrogantly, as he, too, had the *Miami Teen Social* page uploaded on his computer during study hall.

"Dude, I didn't do anything with Emily," Talan said, trying to downplay it. Pictures don't lie, Talan.

"It looks like you kind of did," all the guys said, putting in their two cents worth. Deep down inside, however—unlike his father would have—Talan felt stupid . . . for a while, anyway.

"How could you do this?" Sasha asked Emily heatedly. Wow, so unlike Sasha. Instead of attacking her newfound "love," which would be Talan, she went after a friend she's had for years. Emily didn't even bother denying it, already knowing what she was talking about.

"It's not my fault. One thing just led to another," Emily tried to explain. Not so fast, Emily Parker (who was ecstatic that her name showed up in *Miami Teen Social* and her "star" on the social ladder had risen quite a bit by being in the center of a handsome love triangle). You knew exactly what you were doing.

"You knew that I liked him," Sasha said, trying to maintain her poise, which was just so noble.

"Last night, he sure didn't seem to share the same feelings that you have for him," Emily stated, starved for attention. A small crowd hovered around them.

"You're one of my best friends. How could you do that?" Sasha cried out, losing her composure.

"No, we were friends back in junior high. This is high school, Sasha—can you seriously give me what Talan can?" she replied, almost smirking. Sasha was full-blown crying now.

"Come on, Sasha. You don't need this." Jennifer came by and basically carried her friend away from the drama. However, if Jennifer thought that she and Sasha were going to have "girl time," she was seriously mistaken.

"I have to talk to Talan," Sasha stated right away.

In the A wing, Talan was still being praised for his achievements last night and for landing on *Miami Teen Social*. Talan wasn't one to enjoy being in the tabloids. To a lot of people's surprise, Talan was actually a private person. He was, in fact, in a high emotional state—that was until he saw Sasha Chandler walking (well, more like intensely striding) over toward him. Her face was red, obviously from crying.

"What's wrong?" he asked, already in charming mode.

"What's wrong? Last night after I left, you were with Emily?" she cried out loud. This was the first boy Sasha had actually liked since her stepfather's passing, and Talan Merrick managed to go and obliterate her already fragile heart. Any chances of her opening up with another guy were shot now. Talan looked around to see everyone looking at them. Now, here he was trying to be private about things, when *everyone* knew what was going on. He gently took Sasha's hand and led her outside, where the blazing August sun met them, and it didn't make the situation any better.

"All I did was talk to her," he admitted. Sasha looked deep into his beautiful-manipulating-blue eyes.

"She said that one thing led to another," Sasha naively whispered. Talan was getting annoyed, a combination of both the glaring sun and Sasha's stubbornness.

"Come on! Do you really think that I would try to go after Emily, when I have someone like you?" He cradled her warm face, smiling.

"No."

"See?" he answered; then he came closer and kissed her on her moist lips. Sasha's breath went absent as they kissed. She knew the rumors weren't true, and she also knew that Emily had a thing for Talan. What girl didn't? Even her so-called best friend Johnson had a thing for him. However, Sasha had clearly made the decision of whom she believed—and it was Talan.

Many say, never believe the tabloids. They just make up lies so they can get more views or sell more. As people saw Talan and Sasha walking back into Hamilton Prep hand in hand, they showed their reaction—on tabloid comment spaces. Nevertheless, they said something completely different to their faces.

"I'm so glad you and Talan worked things out," Lorraine told Sasha as they walked to their waiting vehicles after school.

"Thanks. I just knew that Emily was trying to start things. I know they were pictured closely together, but that's all it was. He promised me," Sasha said, smiling as she climbed into the backseat of a Range Rover.

"See you tomorrow," Lorraine said, "smiling." Bet Sasha had no idea that under the article about her in *Miami Teen Social*, there was a comment left by miamihottiegurl that read, "so, so surprised that Talan cheated on her on their very first date! NOT. Ever since her stepfather died, Sasha's just going to end up like her mother. Old, lonely, depressed, and chasing after guys that won't EVER want her!!! Sasha is so fat and ugly it's sad. She'll just peak at high school, if that." Sasha also in all probability had no idea that miamihottiegurl was Lorraine Everly—like we said, betrayal is so sweet when you're fifteen, but then again you are fifteen, so you forget about it like you do everything else. Signing off once again on this exhausting world of reporting on the lifestyles of the privileged and annoying, it's *Miami Teen Social*. We would like to make a shout out to all of our loyal readers, who just *love* to comment on our articles. So we've decided to display your comments from now on in our articles. It's fans like you that keep us in business, but more importantly keep the drama spinning. Until next time . . .

Chapter Four

The Beauty and the Felon

Many people say that beauty is only skin deep, but in a world where beauty and money are everything, why would such a saying come about? We're not all constructed to look like Sasha Chandler or Talan Merrick. Heck, some people aren't even fortunate enough to look like Lily Carrington, and if she were to move to some . . . Brownhole, Indiana, she would look like a supernatural being in her long, glossy auburn hair and innocent round face. Despite being a go-getter and at times annoying, Lily enjoys her fashion just as much as her books. So why is she overlooked by the society of Hamilton Prep? Well, my dear Miss Carrington, the gods, and we're not talking about your father the senator, have heard your cries and have answered.

"Everyone, we have a new student," Mrs. Mulberry announced as an awkward young boy stared at the floor beside her. Hope he knows what he's getting himself into by attending Hamilton Prep. The boy had curly, moppy brown hair, and if he lived in . . . Brownhole, Indiana, could possibly be a pick for homecoming king. "This is Cliff Bowmen, and he transferred here from Cheyenne, Wyoming," she said, smiling. Having a new student in Hamilton Prep was like seeing Sasha Chandler and Talan Merrick making out in the quad—it was attention-grabbing at first, but then students quickly got used to it.

Cliff walked and sat down in the first empty seat he saw—of course right next to Lily Carrington.

"Hi, I'm Lily Carrington, class president . . . well, your president." She giggled awkwardly.

"Hi, it's nice to meet you," Cliff answered, relieved that people were actually polite in the big city of Miami. We undoubtedly imagine that Cliff has no idea of how much of a nightmare it could be in Hamilton Prep if you're not "beautiful." Don't think the cards are in his favor, either.

"Students, today we will be doing some English comp. Get out your notebooks, and jot down some books that you read over the summer," Mrs. Mulberry announced. "Then you will be writing vivid summaries on five of them tomorrow. But after you finish the list, I want you to read the British lit page."

"Does this mean we don't have to turn in that paper on what we did to save energy or what we didn't do to save energy over the summer?" someone in the back row said, smirking. Lily sighed.

"Why would you want to be in advanced English, if you don't want to do the work?" Lily mumbled.

"Exactly," Cliff answered. For a moment, the two looked at each other directly in the eyes. How cute! Lily had never experienced eye sex before. She looked down, feeling awkward and uneasy.

"No, Mr. Monroe. That assignment will still be due by tomorrow, printed, and double-spaced." Her statement was met by a bunch of bitchy moans and groans. Lily swiftly complied and went to work on the new assignment. However, something bothered Lily. She felt something she had felt only when she was around Talan; she couldn't help but look out of the corner of her eye to see Cliff—and Lily had a new crush. As she finished writing her last book down, she took a second to think about why she liked Cliff. He was cute and all, but in the land of Hamilton Prep, which was filled with roses and orchids, he was a wallflower, a dandelion—he was clear. That is precisely why she decided she liked him so much. He didn't hide behind his famous footballer dad or his tycoon family. Maybe Lily Carrington will break the curse of Hamilton Prep students seeing only what's on the outside.

"So are you excited to be living in Miami?" Lily finally asked Cliff as she saw him finish his list.

"Kind of," Cliff answered, a bit tense.

"It's a really cool place to live." Lily's eyes strayed over to his paper, where her eyes met—promise. "Oh, my God, I love *To Kill a Mockingbird.*" As Lily read more of his list, not only did she discover that he read more books then she, but they mostly read the same books.

"We totally—" Lily stopped herself, knowing she had used the stupidest word in her vocabulary, *totally.* "Excuse me. Sorry. What I meant to say is—" Lily was interrupted by the bell. Oh, doesn't that just suck for her. She would have continued, but she had her journalism class, which was a far stretch from her locker, and she didn't want to be late. We all know how overachievers can be. Lily sulked off to her journalism class, upset that she didn't get to fully know Cliff, but then she reminded herself that she was writing an article in her journalism class about new students, so she just smiled.

"We need to hang out tonight," Johnson demanded more than said to Sasha as they sat down on the couch in the lounge area after class. Johnson was amazed that Sasha wasn't vacuuming out Talan's mouth at that moment.

"Talan and I are totally going out to his place tonight. Sorry," Sasha replied, texting.

"We never hang out anymore since you started—" Johnson stopped himself, knowing that he didn't want to upset Sasha, and Sasha could get upset rather quickly. To his dismay, nevertheless, Sasha wasn't even listening—she was texting Talan.

"You bore," Johnson hissed under his breath, knowing Sasha didn't hear him. Well, Johnson, as you insult your best friend, be prepared to be the talk of the school. It seemed that his little rampage a couple nights ago had come back to haunt him.

Everyone gawked at the police as they took Johnson Sinclair to a juvenile detention center on assault charges. Sasha immediately called the same person she always called when Johnson got into trouble, the only person who was there for him—his lawyer.

"OMG, I seriously don't remember the night of these alleged charges." Johnson was being interrogated by the police and a youth detention officer, and in all honesty, he could care less. Johnson was more preoccupied with whose party he should attend—Faiday Hayward's, or Justin Costillo's. He settled for Justin's, since he was a junior, and let's face it, was way hotter than Faiday's. He pictured Justin as the police officer read over his charges. Justin filled Johnson's head. His short black hair, and that right arm of his, which was covered with tattoos. Johnson had always wanted a tattoo, but he thought he was too young . . . yeah, too young for a tattoo, but not too young to throw glasses and party until all hours of the night.

"Mr. Sinclair, are you paying attention?" Yolanda, the youth officer, asked.

"Yeah, whatever. Tell Frizzy Lizzy, I'll pay five grand for the charges to be dropped," Johnson suggested, looking at Berna Mackenzie, his lawyer.

"Now, Mr. Sinclair," the police officer spoke, "assault is a serious charge. You can't just pay if off like some of the other small charges you've had. Miss Elizabeth Van Ryan is adamant about pursuing this in court."

"She just wants the media there so she can get her ugly name out there! My grandfather has had enough of this!" Johnson snapped. Berna cleared her throat.

"Okay, I think my client has had a long day today," Berna stated. Yolanda and the officer both agreed, eager to get the demanding presence of a Sinclair out of there.

After they left the detention center, Berna turned to Johnson on a "serious" note—yeah, right, when do Johnson and serious go together?

"These are very serious charges, Johnson," she repeated. "You have to appear in a teen detention court in a month and a half for this hearing." Berna tried to explain what could happen—fines (which Johnson blew through on a weekly basis), anger management classes, even alcohol classes, close observation by social workers—but Johnson didn't even pay any attention. In many people's opinions, these charges would be a wake-up call for the famous heir, but when you're Johnson Sinclair, why care about anybody's opinion?

Maybe now, since Lily Carrington has found what tickles her toes, she can call herself a beauty because she has something other than her dad's money (or her dad's last name). She's found that certain someone that people get ready for in the morning. The certain someone that makes her feel good. Okay, we know it's only been a day, but when Lily finds something that is worth going for, she goes for it. It seems that nowadays money and status are what make people beautiful or not. Well, we think not. Reporting on the new beauty that is Lily Carrington, who seems to have her life on the right track, unlike so many of the Hamilton Prep students, and also reporting on that felon Johnson Sinclair, who's facing serious charges, but why should we care, if he doesn't. It's *Miami Teen Social.* Goodnight, Miami and fellow readers. Remember, beauty is what you make it, and you can achieve it no matter what. It only takes a certain someone to call you beautiful to make you feel beautiful. That certain someone is the one you love. Please don't throw drinks at anyone. Until next time . . .

Chapter Five

Love or Lust

Are teenagers making out in public and groping each other, and then breaking up five minutes later, in love, or is it lust? Are young adults getting married, and then divorcing a year later, in love or in lust? Does love last, or is lust taking over? For the teens of Hamilton Prep, love is for the moment. They think that they'll last forever, but let's be serious: nothing lasts at Hamilton Prep. It's carpe diem all the time here.

"I almost did it last night," Sasha blurted out as she and Johnson lounged around in the sunny quad in between classes.

"Did what?" Johnson asked as he took a drink from his iced tea.

"You know . . . *it*," Sasha said, almost embarrassed to say the three-letter word.

"Penetration?"

"Johnson, don't say it like that." Sasha giggled, and just then she gulped as she saw Talan walking over. Someone had a tongue-tied night last night.

"Please, I was held up in a mortifying detention center with a bunch of runaways for like two hours. Don't start complaining, because I would have rather spent two hours with Talan than in there. I did go to Justin's party, FYI, and it was fun . . . from what I remember."

"Johnson, please, can you concentrate on me for just once?" Sasha pleaded as Talan made his way over. Johnson nodded. "I totally choked last night. I know we've been slowly making progress, but he . . . I mean, I . . . just . . ." It was too late. Talan had walked over.

"It's hot out here." Talan kissed Sasha on her cheek and sat down next to her.

"Hi. Yeah, it's nice out." Sasha smiled innocently. Talan nodded at Johnson saying hi, and Johnson smiled back. The three sat awkwardly on the bench.

"So . . ." Johnson started, "any plans for tonight?"

"Yeah, Talan and I are going to go to his place and then out on his dad's boat."

"You're welcome to come if you want," Talan added. Johnson had a feeling that Talan didn't really want him to go. Since last night was a total flop, he assumed Talan would probably want another go at it, and Johnson didn't want to be anywhere near them when that happened.

"No, thanks. You guys have fun."

As Lily strolled into her algebra class, she had Cliff on her mind. She couldn't wait until English class when she would get to see him again. Every single time she thought about him, she felt light-headed—and Carringtons never felt light-headed, so she knew she had to get it together. Then, to her absolute surprise, Cliff was sitting in the front row of her algebra class.

"Cliff?" she said, almost speechless.

"Lil." Cliff splattered a goofy smile on his face—how adorable. "I mean Lily," he corrected himself

"I can't believe we have another class together," she stated, shocked. She knew it had to be fate. She quickly sat down next to him.

When class began, Lily boldly looked and smiled at Cliff. Then to her admiration, he smiled back. She couldn't believe it. Lily had never had a boyfriend; the only person she had ever liked before was Talan, but she knew that was never gonna happen. Soon, a note dropped on Lily's desk. Her breath almost skipped a beat. Lily had never passed notes during class. How scandalous. Her hands practically shook as she opened it. In scratchy print it read,

we should do something after school

"I have cello lessons," she said aloud after she read it. Everyone turned to look at her. Mr. Nealey turned around from the chalkboard.

"Oh, I'm very sorry," Lily apologized, embarrassed. As soon as Mr. Nealey turned back around, she quickly wrote in her perfect print,

I have cello lessons

She quickly set the note on his desk. Cliff laughed as he read it.

how about something after then

He set it back down on her desk. Lily was so nervous that she might get caught—but she enjoyed the ecstasy of waiting for what he was going to say.

We could do homework. Once I get done with my cello lesson, we can do homework.

She hastily gave the note back and got back into the world of adjacent, opposite, and exterior angles, until two seconds later when she saw the note had ended up back on her desk.

Sounds good

Lily was as giddy as a young schoolgirl, no pun intended, once she read the note. She smiled during the rest of class.

Just as two Hamilton Prep students would get closer, two others would get farther apart. Johnson was texting on his phone when he rounded a corner in the B wing, and he heard Talan talking (Johnson could detect Talan talking from a mile away), but it was to whom he was talking that made Johnson stop right in his expensive dress shoes—Emily Parker.

"No, Emily. We're done," Talan said.

"Talan, please. You said that we could work." Johnson could hear that Emily was crying, her voice full of desire. He also thought she sounded extremely pathetic.

"It was just that one night, and we almost got caught," he responded, sounding sad, but equally harsh.

"One night? It's been more than one night, Talan!" Emily cried.

"I can't keep lying to Sasha. I want to make things work out with us. It was fun while it lasted, but good-bye, Emily, and stop texting me." Johnson quickly went into a nearby corner as Talan rounded the corner.

What had Johnson just heard? Was Talan cheating on Sasha, his best friend, with his other good friend? Johnson was thinking about it when he ran into Emily.

"Emily," Johnson said, not knowing what to say.

"Hi, Johnson," she sniffled, wiping away at her red face with a paper towel.

"Are you okay?" he asked, sounding more cruel than worried.

"Yeah."

"You don't seem okay."

"Just a long day," Emily replied.

"Oh, well, you still have four more hours until you can go home, and I have a feeling it's going to get worse." Johnson swiftly turned around and went back to class. Ouch, just when Emily Parker couldn't lose any more of her self-respect, it went down a couple notches, thanks to Johnson.

"Sasha." Johnson walked over to Sasha after class.

"Yeah," she replied. Johnson noticed she had a cute bow in her hair, and he was about to comment on it, but shook it off and quickly got back to his little mission.

"There's something I need to tell you."

"Guess who?" Talan said as he as he came from behind Sasha and covered her eyes with his hands.

"Talan," she guessed. Johnson sighed, probably thinking, Stupid blond, who else could it be?

"Correct," Talan answered. Sasha turned around and gave Talan a quick peck on the lips. "I'll talk to you later, Johnson." She grabbed Talan's hand, and they walked down the hall. Johnson's fist clenched in resentment. Let's just hope for Sasha's sake that there are not any glasses around.

"I hope you see it's only lust," Johnson whispered as a couple of his friends advanced toward him.

Lust is for the moment, and love is for life. Is it that young love starts and soon turns to lust, or is it lust from the very beginning? Is Talan

Merrick and Sasha Chandler's first night as an official couple on a romantic boat love or lust? We'll let you decide on that one. What if things start off slowly, such as Lily Carrington is doing with her newfound friendship with Cliff Bowmen? They do homework and talk about books, hobbies, and everything on the planet. They avoid any physical contact. Will it last? Will it be love? Everyone knows that young lust never lasts, but if you treat it tenderly and handle it with care, young lust might blossom into love, and love lasts forever. This is *Miami Teen Social*, until next time . . .

Chapter Six

Parents

What makes a wild child? Is it the people that he hangs around with, or is it the people who raised him? Parenting is hard in this day and age. There are so many problems that parents are faced with—teenagers rebelling, pregnancies, perversion, acting out, bullying. For the parents of the students at Hamilton Prep, they have just chosen different methods of raising their children, which is a far cry from the traditional, modern route.

Ernie Carrington chose the path of a career instead of raising his daughter, Lily. He is now a senator, as we all know. Lily, though, was fortunate enough to have a mother who made sure that her daughter got her homework done, practiced her piano, and attended her cello lessons. On the other hand, behind that perfect façade, Cynthia Carrington was never emotionally connected to Lily. Lily spent a lot of lonely nights after being successful in countless concert rehearsals . . . truly heartbreaking.

Don Merrick chose the bachelor road. He might make it seem in the media that he is an inspirational parent by taking time out of his busy bicep-flexing career to go to his son's sports games, but does the public know that he has emotionally and physically made a monster out of his son? Don has tormented poor little Talan since the boy was young, making him unable to emotionally attach to anything breathing. Behind the handsome face, and the waves of perfect blond hair, lies a cold human being, a teenage boy—a cruel boy.

Don does take some time, if you would call it that, out of his day to see his son, but what about famous heir Roman Sinclair, who has been out of the country for two years? Yep, he just left behind his wife, who was pregnant, and his son. Everyone knows that the mass of the Sinclairs' money is controlled by the patriarch of the family, old Dale Sinclair. Let's just say, Dale has seen better days these last couple of years. With Roman, the eldest of the Sinclair siblings, in hiding (rumors indicate it has to do with Columbian drug lords?), this would make Johnson in the lead of his cousins for a large inheritance when good ol' Grandpa Dale dies. At this instant, that's a lot of money to buy glasses of drinks to throw at people. With his public troubles of partying all night, and most recently assault charge, rumors have been circulating that Grandpa Dale has been threatening to cut Johnson out of the will. Now those are just rumors, but, yikes! If Johnson doesn't straighten up, he could lose all the money. Let's face it, we want Johnson to screw up, and frankly, he will.

Lenny Chandler chose the trail of youth, but she had no idea that she would become pregnant at the age of twenty-one. She was on her way to becoming a supermodel, but a baby got in the way. To her, it was anything but a good thing. Who could blame her—she was young. She wanted to go out, and she had a couple boyfriends—probably too many, since she didn't know who the dad was. That's how Sasha Chandler came about. Lenny loved Sasha, like a little girl would love a puppy . . . she cared about her until she could make messes and get around. Then she just simply dropped Sasha off at her mother's. Lenny tried to get back into modeling, but was damaged goods. Her biggest gig was shooting a commercial about baby diapers. She played the doting mom—how ironic. Then, by chance, she would bump into a man who would change her life. She would get married to the millionaire, demand her child from her mother, and then chuck her off to the nannies. If you looked with your eyes, everything seemed nice, but if you looked twice, you could see it was all lies. The Chandler family was hiding a deep, dark secret that wouldn't portray them as everyone perceived. Brad Chandler died about a year ago, when he tragically fell down a flight of stairs and broke his neck. Lenny turned to the bottle, and she has truly tried being the world's best mom . . . if all parents drank and were crazier than their own children, that is. For the parents of Hamilton Prep students, it is quite difficult to overshadow their children, but Lenny manages to star in the tabloids just as much as her daughter.

It's another weekend for the students of Hamilton Prep, and it seems that all the parents are in town tonight. It's an especially big night for Cliff, as he is meeting Senator Carrington—maybe the couple is getting serious? However, Mommy and Daddy just think that they are going to have dinner with Lily's friend. In all honesty, they would freak if they knew where this relationship was going.

"I'm nervous, Lil," Cliff admitted as they worked on their English essays.

"Don't be, Cliff," she said, smiling. Lily couldn't help but smile when she was around Cliff. When he was around, an undying smile would spread across her porcelain face, and her stomach would do somersaults.

"Well, he's the senator," he replied, worried.

"You met my mom, and she seemed to like you. I think it will be just wonderful, and it's just dinner. How bad could things get?" Guess there wasn't any wood to knock on, because poor Lily jinxed herself, and unfortunately dinner was as awkward as two penguins walking on the beach.

"So, Dad, how was work?" Lily asked while playing with her main dish, which consisted of smoked salmon, and other small overpriced foods.

"Work is work. Did you finish cello lessons? When is your next recital?" he asked, not even bothering to look up from his cell phone.

"Yes, I finished, and my next recital is in a month. Did you hear—"

"I'll make time for it," he cut her off. "Did you accomplish what you wanted, when you suggested they should move the lockers at Hamilton? They didn't make you president of the freshman class for nothing." He took a bite of some steamed rice.

"Mr. Berndt said that it was unlikely to happen, since, I guess, it would mess up the sophomore classes—"

"You guess?"

"Well . . ."

"I have to make a call. Please excuse me, ladies, Cliff." Senator Carrington stood up and walked out of the large dining room. Ruthless, dissing his own daughter in front of her crush.

"This salmon is fantastic. Do you like it, Cliff?" Cynthia blindly asked as her husband left.

"Yes, thank you, Mrs. Carrington, for dinner." Cliff tried to smile, but couldn't, seeing Lily was a little hurt by her father's dealings. Cynthia smiled, oblivious to anything that was going on, and took a sip of her wine. Cynthia was the perfect politician's wife: she was hushed, attractive, graceful, and kept the dirty laundry in the hamper, meaning she kept all secrets sealed, including ill-at-ease dinners.

"Dinner was nice," Cliff said as he lay next to Lily in her room. Even though he'd been in the house a couple times, Cliff was still captivated by the size of the house. Lily's bedroom alone was bigger than his apartment. It was the senator's mansion. What did he expect?

"My father doesn't even care about me," Lily finally confessed. About time, Lil. Even the deaf orphans on the street corner knew that.

"Yes, he does," Cliff tried to soothe her. "It's just that he has to help run Florida, so it's hard for him to keep up with his daughter's extraordinary accomplishments." Cliff smirked. Lily broke a smile and looked at him. A big moment was about to materialize. Cliff leaned in closer—their lips were inches away from each other's. They could feel each other's breath on one another's cheeks . . . It was just too bad Lily was on the edge of the bed. Just as Cliff was finishing leaning in, Lily turned and fell off the bed.

"Ouch!" she cried out. Cliff jumped off the bed and knelt beside her.

"Are you okay?" he asked as he knelt down at her side.

"Yeah, I'm fine," she answered, laughing out. Soon after she stopped laughing, they received another moment. They both gazed into each other's eyes. Lily struggled to take a breath. Then, slowly, ever so slowly, their lips met—yet another accomplishment for Lily. It was a touching and charming split second.

"We could read a book?" Lily suggested afterward.

Football season was in full swing, and Sasha found herself waiting for Talan to get done with practice. Sasha was sitting in the sunny bleachers overlooking the field. All her friends had taken off with Johnson for an afternoon of shopping and eating at fancy cafés. Sasha sat under an umbrella and was wearing full-sized Mary-Kate Olsen bug sunglasses.

"Hey," she heard someone call to her. She looked down to see Jace Costillo, a junior—who had broken his ankle over the summer, and therefore couldn't compete in this season of football—standing by her. She thought about his cousin, Justin, whom Johnson was seriously crushing on. Hell, even she had a small thing for Justin, the bad boy of Hamilton Prep.

"Hey." Sasha smiled back. She questioned why a junior would be talking to her; she slightly tucked her hair behind her ears, knowing she had a striking face. "Sucks not playing football?" she asked. Jace maneuvered his crutches and sat down next to her. His whole foot was in a big black brace.

"Yeah, it totally sucks. So, you and Talan are dating, huh?"

"Yeah," she answered, smiling. "His dad is in town tonight, so we're going to have dinner with him."

"Oh. Well, it was nice to meet you," he said as he held out his hand. Sasha took it and shook it. To her surprise, he brought up her delicate hand and gently kissed it. He then got up.

"Hope to see you around more." Jace smiled, seeing practice was over.

"Yeah."

"Why were you talking to Jace?" Talan demanded, walking out of the locker room after a quick shower.

"I don't know. He came up and talked to me." Sasha tried not to make a problem of the situation, but Talan always made a problem out of the littlest things. He had just become so demanding lately.

"Well, you shouldn't be talking to anyone. You should be watching me." They walked over to Talan's limo, which his dad had sent for him. It was a reminder that he was in town.

"Sorry?" Sasha suggested, thinking back to when they first started dating, and he was with Emily, whom she hadn't talked to in a while. They both got in.

"Thanks," Sasha said to the driver opening the door for them.

"Yeah, whatever," Talan muttered as he slouched down on the seat, and pulled out his phone and started texting.

Once Talan and Sasha arrived at his condo on the gated island of Brickell Key, just off of Miami's financial district Brickell, they saw Don Merrick in the kitchen mauling a woman who wasn't his girlfriend. The woman, who looked drop dead gorgeous, was wearing short capris and a belly-baring top.

"You can wait in my room," Talan told Sasha. She nodded and walked down the hallway and turned into his bedroom.

"Dad," Talan stated, quite loudly.

"Oh." Don stopped. "Claudia, this is my son, uh, Talan." He walked over.

"It's nice to meet you, Talan," Claudia greeted him in a foreign accent. By the way she looked, Talan could already tell she was some supermodel from Brazil.

"Pleasure's all mine," he replied blankly.

"Claudia, can you please excuse us?" Don asked Claudia.

"Yeah, I'll wait by the pool." She kissed Don before exiting the room. Talan watched her as she strutted out to the large balcony. She took off her top to reveal a bathing suit.

"So, how's it been going?" Don asked his son as he prepared two martinis, for him and Claudia, of course.

"Good. Sasha is here; we were going to have dinner together. Remember?" Talan said, almost trying to get his dad's approval.

"Shoot," Don swore. He thought for a second. "Sounds perfect for a barbecue." He was leaving the room until he passed Talan, "Are you doing those workouts I gave you to do?" He evaluated his son's form.

"I've tried, but with football starting, and with Sasha, it's hard to fit in enough time."

"Hey, listen," Don interrupted him. He stepped closer to his son. "You come first. So put away everything else." He patted his son's cheek—maybe a little too hard.

"Okay," Talan replied coldly, his cheek slightly red.

"So what are we going to do?" Sasha asked as Talan came into his room. She was sitting on his bed texting.

"I dunno." Talan walked over and started to kiss her passionately.

"What do you mean, you 'dunno'?" she asked.

"It means I don't know," Talan snapped. "God, I'm just kidding." Talan smiled and started kissing her neck. Bipolar, anyone?

After a relatively fun barbecue dinner, which went smoothly, Sasha got to know Don, and really liked him. Talan got to see more of Claudia (possibly his future stepmom), as she changed into another barely-there bikini and jumped into the pool out on the huge balcony overlooking the rest of Brickell Key, and the surrounding ocean.

"See you tomorrow." Sasha kissed Talan.

"Okay," he said as he led her to the elevator. It was sometime around one in the morning, and Sasha had really enjoyed herself. She knew that her mom was still out. Sasha walked out of the colossal-sized condo complex, which looked like it went all the way up to heaven, and she jumped into an awaiting vehicle. Sasha took a deep uneven breath; she felt like the condo was heaven.

"Mom!" Sasha almost scolded, seeing her mom making out with some guy on the sofa in the living room as she arrived home.

"Oh, Sasha!" Lenny jumped off. "I thought you were sleeping."

"No, I just got back from Talan's."

"I got you some things today," she said as she handed Sasha a couple of bags filled with Gucci slacks and blazers. Sasha looked behind her to see the man putting his shirt back on. "It's for this formal luncheon next week." She smiled, waving it away. Sasha looked at her mom. Her hair was disheveled, and her makeup was smeared. Without saying anything, she walked up to her room. She dumped the clothes on her bed and rummaged through them. The blazers were really great. She loved them. She set them aside and changed, washed off her makeup, and jumped into bed. Soon, she heard the door open, and someone kissed her cheek. It was her mom.

"Oh, Sasha, I'm sorry. If I knew you were still out, I wouldn't have brought anyone home." Sasha turned to face her mother.

"It's okay." Sasha touched her mother's hand. Her mother's smile faded, and a frown sprung up.

"It's just . . . it's hard without your stepfather here. They said he was drinking when he fell down those damn stairs," she cried, trying to be strong. Sasha hated it when her mother brought up her stepfather.

"I'm tired."

"Okay, sweetie. Goodnight." Lenny kissed Sasha goodnight before leaving. That night, Sasha cried herself to sleep. The only thing that helped was when she called Talan. He got mad at her for waking him up, and unfortunately, he didn't have any advice for her. He just told her everyone, except for him, fought with his or her parents. He suggested she grow up and be strong. Despite the harsh facts, she agreed with him. Wow, it looks like Sasha is truly in love. Her last words to him before hanging up were, "I love you." His last words: "I know. Goodnight."

The next day, Johnson Sinclair was being driven to meet with his grandfather Dale. He was happy that he was going to get to see his busy grandpa regardless of his recent troubles. They were meeting for lunch at Cacao, which is an elegant place right in Johnson's little town of Coral Gables, and a prominent spot for Hamilton Prep students to have lunch with their families.

"Grandpa," Johnson greeted him, dressed in his best attire of a light red Burberry sweater with a striped button-down under it. To finish off, he was wearing black slacks. It looked like he had gotten into a fight with a candy cane.

"Johnson." The old man smiled and tried to get up, but his hips were a little sore. He had already replaced them twice. Dale had a man dressed in a suit next to him, one of his handlers. Johnson came up and gave the old man a peck on the cheek before sitting down.

"Have you heard from your father?" Dale asked, as if his son had left just a week ago.

"No, Grandpa, I haven't heard from Roman," Johnson replied. An appealing waiter dressed in a typical white shirt and black slacks approached them.

"Oh, yes," Dale started. "I will have the steakhouse and an iced tea." Dale didn't even bother looking at the menu. He was one of those people who knew what they wanted and never changed their minds, one of the reasons his company was so successful, and another reason why his family never got along.

"I would like an iced tea and the Caesar salad." Johnson smiled. The waiter nodded and left.

"What's this? Mr. Caulfield was telling me the other day about a Ms. Van Ryan pressing assault charges against you?" he said almost in a hushed voice. Johnson rolled his eyes, knowing that his grandpa didn't see very well.

"I absolutely have no idea, Grandpa. I was with my friends, and next thing I knew, someone threw a drink, and I heard Lizzy scream." The waiter soon returned with their drinks.

"Thank you." Johnson smiled overdramatically—God, this was like a cheesy soap.

"Johnson, I'm really tired of hearing about you getting into trouble. Roman was supposed to take over the company, when, God forbid, I pass, but it's almost fallen to you." Johnson almost choked on his drink.

"What? Run Sinclair Corp.? Are you kidding me? What about Aunt Maria, or Aunt Rosie, or don't you like have some cousin that can do it?" Johnson could run the company—straight into the ground, and he knew it. Johnson didn't want to have a job once he graduated from Hamilton. He didn't even know if he was going to college. College, Johnson thought, was for working-class people, and those were the worst kind of people.

"No. Rosie and Maria have made it very clear that they want to raise their children, and if they take over the company, it's going to make that virtually impossible. I should know."

"I'm only fifteen," Johnson reminded his grandpa, scared he was going senile. Dale sighed heavily.

"Of course, I know that, but I have plans. I've arranged that after you graduate from college, you'll be taking over," he stated seriously. Johnson was, for once in his life, speechless. He opened his mouth but didn't know what to say.

"I don't think I can, Grandpa. I don't even—"

"We're Sinclairs, damn it," Dale hissed. "We can do whatever we want." Dale didn't know that Johnson was going to finish by saying, "I don't even want to run it." "And if you get into trouble one more time, I will have no other choice, but to—he then spoke the words that Johnson had never heard before—"cut you off." Johnson's heart dropped, and his mouth slightly opened. The waiter came by and gave them their food, and Johnson was not even concerned that the waiter saw him looking all down in the dumps, with his jaw open and fear and fret in his eyes.

"Thank you." Dale smiled as the waiter left. "Maybe you should move in with me, so I can keep a better watch over you. After all, you are the new successor to Sinclair Corp., and I need to start molding you."

"I like my house."

"Your mother and little Camber are where . . . Paris?" Dale started on his steak.

"Yes."

"See, you're all alone in that big house—"

"I have Theresa, and the maids," Johnson cut in. Dale managed to let out a small chuckle.

"The maids? Please, Johnson, I'm serious. You should consider moving into The Manor with me." The Manor, which was known as the Sinclair

Mansion to all of Miami society, was where Sinclair formal events were held. It was extremely extravagant and full of lavish, inestimably valuable family heirlooms. Johnson knew that if he were to move into The Manor, his freedom would be over, despite the residence being enormous.

"My mother said she would be coming back soon, and is considering staying in Miami for the better part of the year," he lied through his teeth.

"Oh, really?"

"Yes, Grandpa, and I promise, I will try to fix things."

"That's what I like to hear. Now, eat your salad."

Once lunch was over, Johnson decided to give Lizzy a call so they could talk things over, but of course, he wasn't going alone.

"So sorry," Sasha spoke to Johnson over the phone. "I made plans with Talan already. We were going to go to his place to watch DVDs."

"You know, it's fine. I'll just call someone else," Johnson said as he unemotionally hung up. He decided to call his new best friend—Emily Parker. Is a new friendship emerging, and an old one vanishing?

"Thanks for coming, bitch," Johnson greeted Emily with credit cards in tow. Retail therapy perhaps?

"You're very much welcome, homo." The pair decided to hit up some shopping districts down in Miami Beach, and still being teens, they went to the mall.

"Thanks, I really needed this," Johnson told Emily as they walked, sipping on their double mocha Frappuccinos.

"Yeah, so did I. Lorraine and Jen are like all weird around me now," Emily informed him. Johnson's handlers were walking behind them with tons of bags.

"Oh, let's hit up Burberry," Johnson cheered.

"Okay," Emily replied, giggling.

"This would look fantastic on you." Johnson handed Emily a pair of stretched leather leggings.

"They would, but look at the price. They're almost $1,500," she wheezed. "I've already blown through my pocket money." She laughed as she set them down.

"Burberry is on me." Johnson smiled as he handed her back the leather leggings.

"Thanks." She went to try them on. Along with the leggings, Johnson bought Emily a leather pencil skirt. Emily was still going for her signature look—rocker tramp. Skinny jeans went for $295. Johnson also bought himself a couple polo shirts, various Burberry sweaters, and of course a famous Burberry trench coat worth $1,695.

"Ready to meet Frizzy Lizzy?" Johnson asked Emily once they had everything in Johnson's limo, which Dale so graciously had let him borrow for the day. There's nothing like teaching your grandson a lesson, and then afterward lending him your limo.

"Let's tell this frizzled freak off," Emily said, snickering. They were meeting Miss Van Ryan at a little café down in South Beach.

"Lizzy." Johnson saluted with a fake hug as soon as he saw her.

"Johnson." She smiled back.

"This is my friend Emily. I'm sure you've heard of her." Johnson showed off his entourage.

"So, I don't have much time, so I was just wondering if I gave you $5,000 could this all be resolved, and could you just drop the charges. Then we can just go on ignoring each other," Johnson proposed.

"No," Lizzy merely responded.

"No?" Johnson looked at Emily for any ideas.

"I want this to proceed. You see, it's a way of getting my name out there, and if I want to rise in the quote/unquote "social ladder," then a fiasco like this would be perfect. Don't you think?" She smiled vindictively. Johnson, on the other hand, lost his temper.

"Listen, you freak, your family has sucked more money and blood in this town than a backstreet dentist, so get lost, you whore!" For a moment, it looked as if he were going to take a plate and hurl it at her.

"Johnson!" Emily held him back. "Not here. Let's go." Emily escorted her dear friend from the premises, leaving a visibly shaken Lizzy Van Ryan working out the crocodile tears for everyone to see.

What makes a wild child? Is it absent parents or brutal parents? If Johnson Sinclair's father wouldn't have left the country and stayed to care for his son, would he be acting out in a public place? If Senator Carrington would have congratulated his daughter more, would she still be striving to please him, no matter what the cost? If Don Merrick would have told his son, "I love you" more, would Talan have been more human? What if Lenny Chandler had been there more for her daughter when she needed her the most? Would Sasha still be blinded by love? Nonetheless, these are all what-ifs. This is the real world, and in the real world you have to play with the cards you are dealt. Thanks for reading. Until next time, it's *Miami Teen Social* . . .

Chapter Seven

Sick Days and Court Days

Hamilton Prep students coming back from an exasperating weekend and returning to dreary school is like parolees going back to jail. They whimper and complain the whole way, but, sorry to say, unlike the parolees, there aren't officers to make sure it gets done. Too often they are "sick" and stay in their lavish homes resting from the heavy weekend.

> Behind her regal exterior, Sasha Chandler seems to be more like her mother; tacky and wild! She reportedly left boyfriend Talan Merrick's house in the wee hours of the morning over the weekend on Friday. Earlier that day, she attended a barbecue with Talan's father and his new girlfriend of the week, Brazilian model Claudia Lago. If she keeps this act up, she will end up like her mother, and have a child at twenty-one! She will then probably drop it off at her mom's house, and it will be taken away by social services. Hopefully, anyway.

> Comments~

> DJ-Deb says—Oh, jezzuss!!! I thought Sasha was one of those girls at Hamilton that was a goody girl, but now she's out at all hours of the night acting wild! She's just like the rest of them.

40

<u>DonniGG</u> says—Give her a break. She's young, and so what if she wants to go out. You guys need to stop picking on kids. You guys are lame and need to get lives!!!

"Someone had a busy night." Johnson laughed Monday morning as he lay in his bed all morning drinking tea and reading *Miami Teen Social*. (Guess he's secretly a fan.) "Huh, Chutney?" He played with his pet chinchilla, who was growing her fur back. Little did Johnson know there was an equally scandalous article about him, and his ex-bestie, Sasha, was reading it.

Johnson Sinclair is at it again. After having lunch with his old grandpappy, mega real estate mogul Dale Sinclair, Johnson hit up Miami Beach. He took in some superfluous retail therapy, with new bestie Emily Parker. Guess he and Sasha have finally split. Frown face. The pair hit up stores like Burberry, where they blew through a staggering $4,680! So much for those rumors of cutting Johnson off, right? That was just the beginning of the day. Soon, they met up with Frizzy Lizzy. Yes, Frizzy Lizzy Van Ryan, who just recently pressed charges against the famous heir for assault. Any hope for reconciliation was dashed when Johnson and Frizzy Lizzy had yet another heated argument. Luckily, there weren't any glasses around, and Johnson left shortly after. Johnson is due in court in a while, and we wonder what will happen. Just please, make him go away, judge!!

Comments~

<u>K!KI</u> says—I only wish that Johnson could go away and never come back! He is so annoying!! His grandpa should donate his inheritance to some charity for a good cause

41

and not have him blowing through five grand a day!!!! He is a waste.

"Johnson, it's Sasha. I was just calling because I read the article about you in *Miami Teen Social*, and I'm a little worried about you. You're acting pretty crazy, and I don't think Emily is a good influence on you right now. Okay, so call me when you can." Johnson purposely ignored Sasha's call. Sasha had decided that today she needed some personal Sasha time, and was watching reruns of *The Golden Girls*, while texting Talan, eating low-fat ice cream, and drinking water. Maybe she's watching her weight?

Talan took a while to respond to Sasha's texts because he had missed school, so he could catch up on his grueling workout schedule. I bet a bunch of teen girls would just love to see Talan shirtless, working out in his home gym—well, sorry, ladies. We report, not stalk. Big difference.

"Come on, Talan," Don coached as Talan worked with more and more pressure building on him. We wish we had dads who would let us miss school just so we could work out. Once Talan got done with sit-ups, he threw a couple punches at the punching bag. He probably pretended that the punching bag was his dad. When Talan had breaks, he would quickly send one or two words in response to the novel of texts Sasha would write. Then, he'd watch ESPN or eat.

Lily was the only one who was actually sick. She lay in bed with a fever, and her poor little face all red. Perhaps it was from playing tonsil hockey with Cliff over the weekend?

"Do you need anything, Miss Lily?" Cindy, her maid, asked.

"Maybe just some orange juice. I have to keep my fluids up," she informed the maid with a smile on her face. When Cindy came back, Lily took a sip from the glass and looked at the clock—it was 10:01, meaning class was over and a break was in session at Hamilton. Lily got her cell phone and called her beau, whom she missed so dearly.

"Hey, Cliffy." She smiled, knowing he couldn't see how ghastly she looked with her long, dark auburn hair all matted, and without a hint of makeup on her sweaty face.

"Hey, Lil," he replied, sounding happy to hear her voice. "Are you any better?"

"No, not really. I've just been in bed all morning. I tried to read another scene from *Romeo and Juliet*, but my heart just isn't in it."

"It's okay. Just get better, because I really miss you."

"I miss you too. I'll call you during another break. Bye."

"Bye." Lily hung up the phone feeling one hundred degrees better. Good for her.

Johnson Sinclair I think that it's funny when a friend who you cared about so much completely ignores you, then tries to become friends with you, knowing she only has one person in her life that doesn't really care about her.

Sasha was in a state of absolute uncertainty (almost like one time when she couldn't decide on whether to go to a Burberry sale or a Gucci sale. She was so stressed out she left). After reading Johnson's Facebook status, she got out her phone and decided to be the "bigger" person and text her ex-best friend.

Hey, who are you talking about on your facebook? U didn't go 2 school either? LOL we're too much alike.

The message took exactly twenty-three seconds to reach Johnson's phone. And to this, Sasha received,

o we're talking now?

Boy, this time Sasha was even more confused, almost like she was at a Burberry, Gucci, *and* Prada sale all on the same day.

what do u mean? What's wrong??

Johnson could already tell he was going to roll his eyes when he received the text, and sure enough, he did. The pour soul decided to let it out.

Tired of being pushed out of the way because all you want to do is spend time with Talan all the time.

Sasha cracked a smile when she read Talan's name.

43

I'm sorry. It's just we're getting really serious, and he gets me more than anyone else does. He really does.

Johnson almost hurled his phone across his spacious bedroom when he read the "he gets me more than anyone else does" part. He replied as Johnson does to everything else.

Whatever

Sasha got frustrated with Johnson's "whatever". It seems that the word "whatever" really does grind people's gears. Sasha decided to follow in Johnson's footsteps and let her frustrations run free.

You swapped me for Emily, and that really hurt. You know I don't like her and you guys are always together.

Johnson took a deep breath as he read the text. With that, his reply was a lie, and he knew it.

Emily is true friend. She's not fake like some people

Sasha had the final straw. She hated Emily, and now she was starting to dislike Johnson more and more. So she took it to her Facebook:

Sasha Chandler I am SO in love with Talan! Getting to see who my true friends are, and people need to start paying for their actions!!

Someone is certainly sensitive about Johnson going to court soon, but at least we know how she feels about Talan.

"So, after yelling at me, he angrily threw a drink at me." It was the day of the court hearing, and Frizzy Lizzy was reciting the events that had occurred that horrible night. Let's just say that Miss Van Ryan most definitely has a career in acting in her future. She was working the judge with her waterworks. Nonetheless, she was a little overdressed for a court hearing: she was wearing a stunning Armani blazer, with stilettos.

"Thank you, Miss Van Ryan," the judge said, almost comforting her. Johnson rolled his eyes. Miracle of miracles, Johnson's mom, Nicollet, showed up.

"Please rise, Mr. Sinclair." Johnson stood up. "I am very disappointed in you. Such behavior, and you belong to such a prominent family." The overweight judge frowned. "I order you to pay $500 in fines, stay away from Miss Van Ryan, and take anger management classes for two months."

"Anger management!" Johnson blurted out. Berna, his lawyer, almost choked.

"Johnson," she hissed, "zip it."

"Actually, Mr. Sinclair, you're lucky that's all I'm doing. I could have sentenced you to probation. I even could have made you spend time in a juvenile detention center. You're getting off easy."

"Ms. Van Ryan, do you have anything to say about Johnson's sentencing?" a reporter asked Frizzy Lizzy as she left the detention center. She, of course, cued the "tears."

"I'm just glad this is all behind me, and I can rest easier knowing that Johnson Sinclair can't be near me. I would like to thank my family for supporting me during this hard time."

Soon, the reporters reached Johnson and asked him what he thought about his sentencing. He replied in that loud, obnoxious voice of his, "*Buzz off!*"

When Hamilton Prep students stay home from school sick, drama always pursues. Whether it's a struggling friendship or a demanding workout, something always happens in the lives of Hamilton Prep students. It's apparent that this is only the start of this school year, and so much more is to happen. Until next time, it's *Miami Teen Social . . .*

Chapter Eight

Cotillion

A cotillion is when an elite young lady presents herself to society. At Hamilton Prep, the month of November is cotillion week. Of course all the "ladies" are members of the Miami Beach Country Club, which is an exclusive—and might we mention quite expensive—club to be a member of. All the ladies are called debs, which is the "it" thing to call debutants. Cool, right? Cotillions cost tens of thousands of dollars to create, but when you're a Hamilton Prep girl, the more money you spend, the more in style you are.

"So, I was thinking, we should all go dress shopping for the cotillion after school," Emily suggested as she, Lorraine Everly, Jennifer Henderson, and the king bee himself, Johnson Sinclair, all ate at their table during lunch period. Johnson had, in fact, taken over the small freshman scene. Sasha could care less, though, as Talan and his activities now took up her time.

"I think that's a fantastic idea," Lorraine chimed in while leaving comments on *Miami Teen Social* about Sasha or whomever else she was jealous of.

"We should extend an olive branch and maybe invite Sasha," Jennifer suggested politely. Johnson shot his head up.

"Someone has been taking her mom's meds, because your brain cells are completely insensitive," Johnson informed Jennifer.

"It was just a thought," Jennifer replied serenely.

"Yeah, a dumb one," both Emily and Lorraine stated at the same time.

"I can't believe she has the balls to have her cotillion at the country club. Ever since her stepdad died, everyone just pities her and her whore mother. It's pathetic," Emily added. Sasha has completely cut herself off from her friends by being with Talan more. It's just been one big, messy catfight. Emily Parker has definitely emerged as the new "it" girl, by being Johnson's sidekick—how fabulous.

"Let's talk about escorts, ladies," Johnson started in.

"Are you excited?" Cliff asked Lily as they ate lunch outside by an oak tree with a couple of their friends—yes, it's true, Lily actually has made friends, even though they are mostly Cliff's new friends.

"Yeah, are you excited to be my escort?" Lily smiled while fiercely holding on to Cliff's hand.

"Of course," Cliff said as he gave Lily a quick kiss on her cheek. She giggled with happiness.

"My mom and I are going to pick out a dress today." Cliff smiled, happy for her. "What shade of white?" Lily asked, pondering the age-old question of cotillion dresses.

"Ivory," Cliff fished right out of her mind.

"Sounds perfect." Lily leaned against Cliff's curly hair.

Cotillion dresses were the last thing on Talan's mind as he zoned out in history class. He knew that, of course, he was going be Sasha's escort and all eyes were going to be on him—well, Sasha, too, but more on him.

"Mr. Merrick, are you paying attention?" Mr. Kline, the overweight history teacher, asked.

"Yeah," he replied, without even bothering to look up from the window he was gazing out. Wonder what he's looking at? Oh, of course, the cheerleaders.

"Why don't you just display a little outline of the French Revolution then?"

"Okay." Talan strode up to the chalkboard, where to everyone's surprise he started on an accurate time line. Everyone looked at Talan like he was writing out the cure for AIDS. Once he finished, he turned to Mr. Kline, just as Mr. Kline reached for the chalk. Talan dropped it, making it descend to the floor and splinter into a dozen tiny pieces. Not even the least bit worried about how rude he had just acted, Talan walked back to his desk and continued looking out the window.

Cotillion dresses were usually Prada, Gucci, or, of course, Armani. You know, the kinds of dresses that cost more than what Average Joes make in half a year. And Hamilton Prep king bee Johnson has no problem telling a girl that a $15, 000 dress looks bad on her.

"If your hips weren't so big, you would actually look pretty decent in that dress," he told Lorraine. He would also add his point of view on what pair of $750 Christian Louboutin shoes made their feet look clunky.

"God, Emily, you have Paris Hilton feet," he said insultingly.

"I wonder who the slore is shopping with." Lorraine smirked as she tried to constrict her size six waist into a size two corset dress.

"That dress is ass-ugly for a cotillion, Lorraine, and it's not even white," Johnson "kindly" informed her just as he received a text from the slore in question.

hey, what are u guys doin?

"I don't think so. I mean you are right, it's not for cotillion, and it's only five grand, but it makes an amazing party dress," Lorraine said, smiling. She turned to Chancy, the assistant serving them, and scowled. "I want this dress."

They're gettin dresses 4 cotillion. Talan busy?

Johnson sent the message. "I'm just completely in love with this dress," Jennifer, the only one with a heart present, said, beaming. She was wearing a pearl-colored dress with white satin gloves, which were tradition with cotillion dresses. Jennifer's long black hair cascaded down the back of the gown, making for a breathtaking pictorial shoot.

"You look good," were the words from Johnson that made Jennifer feel secure that she would look amazing at the cotillion. Soon, Johnson's phone buzzed with a text from Sasha.

He was at football practice. I would have gone with you guys if you would have asked me to.

Johnson sighed and simply said aloud, "No one wanted to ask you." In the end Emily choose a similar pearl-colored dress that was a measly nine grand. Lorraine walked out with her party dress and an off-white curving gown, charging a costly $17,500 on Daddy's credit card.

"Do I look good, Mom?" Lily asked her mother as she stood in a white gown on a pedestal with five mirrors screaming back at her that she looked perfect.

"Yes, you do, Lily. I just love it, and we can put a lily, or even an orchid in your hair," Cynthia suggested as she walked up and tried to pin her daughter's long hair up.

"Cliff is going to love it." Lily grinned as she twirled around. Lily must have tried on about sixteen white dresses before settling on one, and every single time she asked herself if Cliff would like it. Jeez, Lily's acting as if she were choosing a wedding dress; except for the price of her cotillion dress, it sure did scream wedding dress.

As Sasha's dress got wrapped up, Sasha didn't know what was more disappointing—not being with Talan, or being left out by her former friends. She had to go shopping all by herself. Her own mother was too busy. Yeah, there's a first for everything. She still wanted to be with her friends, but at the same time she wanted to constantly be around Talan. She wanted to have her cake and eat it too. Sasha, my dear, you can't have everything.

"What's wrong? You don't like the dress? It's faboo," Marky, her personal shopping advisor, said.

"No, no, I like it. It's just . . ." The thing about personal shopping advisors was that there really wasn't a personal chip in them, only a shopping one. "Never mind." In her mind she finished, *I just miss my friends.*

"Okay, ladies and gentlemen," Lydia Birchett announced. Tonight was the night of cotillion rehearsal, and nobody wanted to go. As they leaned against the walls texting, eye-rolling, and head-twisting, Lydia Birchett directed the rehearsal. When it came to cotillion parties Lydia was the go-to planner . . . she had been in the business of pleasing demanding, overprivileged snots for years. "Your fathers"—Sasha's head popped up from Talan's neck once she heard the word *father*—"will lead you across the stage, and we'll introduce you. Then he'll give you away to your escort."

To Sasha's relief, someone asked the question she had been dying to ask: "What if we don't currently have a father?"

"That's fine. If you don't have a father, then ask maybe an uncle, older brother, or just a close older male in your life." Lydia continued, "I hope you girls have your dresses." That sentence alone made the quiet room erupt with talk about dresses.

"Excuse me. Lydia tried to calmly break the endless chatter about dresses. "Please pay attention. Here is an outline of some of the billing you will have to talk to your parents about. I know from past experiences it won't get done, so I have printed it out." She started to hand out papers with prices on them. Let's just take a look at how much cotillions cost: around $5,000 goes to catering services, another $3,400 goes to waiters and provided extras such as how you want your waiters to look. Of course, these young elite ladies take full advantage of that. Another $4,000 will let you have the country club for a night, $6,200 is a rough estimate for decorations and other ornamental objects, and the most important thing, the band of your dreams, will run about $12,000. And Mrs. Lydia Birchett charges $2,000 per girl. So the price for such an event will be around $30,000, and just for one shallow night.

After countless walks across the stage, it was clear that nobody wanted to spend another second in the dining hall. Talan was about ready to leave, with Sasha right behind him. Lily already had made up a polite excuse on how her father, the senator (she was going to clear her voice a little when she said that word to Mrs. Lydia), wanted her home early. Johnson was . . . Wait, why was Johnson there?? He wasn't an escort, but maybe he just wanted to keep a close eye on things.

"All right, that's it. Please put your cellular phones in this bedazzled basket," Lydia told them as she toted around a fancy sparkly pink basket with the words "cell phones" bejeweled on it. Everyone made a face as if Lydia were asking for a handout, and then angrily dropped their phones in the basket. "If you girls aren't going to pay attention, then I'm going to take away the reason why you aren't paying attention."

"God, I'm going to vomit if I have to see Sasha mount Talan one more time," Emily murmured into Johnson's ear. A definite deb is still bitter over a breakup. "Look at her. She's so, like, anorexic-looking. Nobody wants that." Emily basically cried as she tucked her long black bob haircut behind her ears.

"I know," Johnson said, so over the conversation.

"I have to go to the bathroom."

"Don't throw up."

"This is starting to get a little boring," Cliff whispered into Lily's ear. She laughed as his breath tickled her ear.

"I know," she agreed. She kissed him on his cheek and giggled with bliss. Lily was in love, completely.

Even though love and friendship were in the air, nobody wanted to stay at the country club any longer. Then, finally, not soon enough, Lydia said the words everybody had been dying to hear:

"Okay, children, you can wait out in the front lobby, and I'll return your cellular phones. I have to make a quick call, and please be careful with this door," she advised as she tried to wedge the door leading out of the dining room area. Slowly, all the "children" made their way out.

"Sasha," Jace addressed her as he ran into her. Talan was busy talking to a couple of his buddies. Is this drama we smell in the air?

"Jace," she said, basically applauding, "I was hoping you would have said something before we left."

"Of course. I wouldn't have just left without saying anything." He rebuilt his posture with his crutches, trying to appear tall and commanding, trying to impress Sasha. His dark blond, almost brown hair was tucked under a cap. Lydia had told him to take it off a dozen times, but when she wasn't looking, he would put it back on. We all thought his cousin Justin was the rebel.

"What have you been up to?" Sasha started, eager to talk to a male other than Talan.

"Nothing much since I've got these." He smirked as he lifted up one of his crutches. Sasha giggled, watching him as he struggled without it. "What about you?"

"Cheerleading, and—"

"Sasha." They both turned to see Talan, of course. The engaging rendezvous was cut short.

"I'll talk to you later." Sasha tried to smile, but this time Sasha couldn't, not with that look on Talan's face, anyway. Sasha walked by Talan's side and followed him to a corner by the stage.

"What the hell is wrong with you?" he gritted.

"Nothing. I was just being friendly, Talan," Sasha mumbled.

"How? By sleeping with the other escorts?" he asked. Sasha's jaw dropped, and her eye's filled with tears. Gosh, it looked like that's all she did—cry and cry.

Meanwhile, Johnson was getting his bag full of clothes. He and Emily were going to have a slumber party. We're pretty sure that Sasha was going to be one of the hot topics for the night, and Johnson was heading for the door.

Lily stood admiring the stage; it almost made her Gucci heels attach themselves to the polished wooden floors. She couldn't move, imagining her dad walking her across the stage, and then giving her to Cliff. She smiled, hoping the moment would be as perfect as it seemed. Only one small noise interrupted everybody . . . *click.* Johnson walked toward the door and tried to open it. To his utter amazement, what Mrs. Lydia had said about being careful with the door slipped his mind entirely. He tried to open the door at least five times before Lily snapped him back to reality.

"Oh, Johnson, try pulling it?" she kindly suggested as she walked over.

"I have!" Johnson crossly replied. Lily almost did a double take when the harshness of his tone hit her ears, but then she smiled as Lily always did.

"What the hell is wrong with the doors?" Talan walked over.

"They won't open," Johnson replied, only too happy to talk to him. Talan walked right over and just about tackled the doors—to his shame, the doors wouldn't shift.

"Everyone left already to go get their phones," Johnson explained to Talan.

At that moment all four children knew that they were stuck in the dining hall until someone opened the doors. It could be an hour, or it could be five minutes, but no matter what the time, one thing was for sure—awkwardness and D-R-A-M-A were sure enough going to fill up the seconds it took for someone to open the doors. The lovely squad splintered, and each had thoughts about the others. As Talan glared into Sasha's eyes, he thought, *Slut*. Ouch! He turned away and walked to a chair and sat down and planted his face into his hands. Sasha turned to Johnson, and her glossy eyes forced out, *Backstabber*. Johnson turned around and right away was face to face with Lily, and his thought: *Twit*. He walked away and leaned against the wall until he slowly slid down and sat on the floor. Lily stood awestruck as she saw Talan sitting down on the chair with his perfect face buried within his hands and arms. She only thought, *OMG*.

"Talan," Sasha mumbled as she approached him.

"What?" he muttered.

"I don't want to fight."

"Then stop talking to other people," he blandly replied. Sasha tried to swallow a big lump in her throat, but she couldn't. She felt her face get red, and she felt stupid.

"I'll just let you cool off." For once Sasha left and was not right by Talan's side.

"Hey," Lily greeted Johnson as she approached him slouched down on the floor. Johnson looked up while Lily elegantly sat down next to him. "I can't wait for cotillion. It's just such an important time for a young girl. It's almost like a marriage, but instead of committing to a husband you're committing yourself to society."

"Ha," Johnson interrupted her. "What society? I've never seen you go out before in my life."

"Society isn't all about going out to parties and getting smashed with fancy Cosmos and martinis, or going out spending thousands of dollars on clothes, Johnson," she tried to explain like she would to a normal, rational person, which Johnson was not.

"Then what is it? If I were like you and just stayed home, I would be a nobody. I have a name to keep up with. I have values." The look on Lily's face was that of consideration (God knows why), but it looked like Johnson was about to hear a wise word from Miss Carrington.

"The only reason people care about you is because of your name. You give people something to talk about, and it's all at the expense of your family. What will your little sister think when she sees you completely acting a mess at four in the morning? But most of all, Johnson, you're just hurting yourself." There you go. Wise, wise words from a young lady who's going places.

Johnson's response . . . "Leave me alone, Lily." Johnson got up and walked to the center of the room. And from there, he saw Talan. Johnson grew weak in the knees when he saw him. He loved everything about Talan; only one voice ruined it.

"Hey, Johnson," Sasha said. Johnson sighed.

"What?"

"Johnson, we were such good friends. What is going on?" Sasha was losing it. Her boyfriend was completely angry at her, and her ex-best friend was annoyed by her.

"You choose your boyfriend over your friends," he clarified. Like Johnson wouldn't have.

"No, I don't. I love Talan, and I want to be with him. I feel like you guys completely hate me for being with him. Emily and Lorraine have boyfriends, and you don't ostracize them." Who would have known Sasha had such a wide range of vocabulary?

"But that's different." Johnson tried to pull off. Was it? Emily had the on-again, off-again thing with Faiday Hayward, and Lorraine switched boyfriends like she did her shoes. Jennifer's boyfriend since fifth grade recently moved away over the summer, and she wanted to be single for a while like a good girl. There was a difference between all the others and Talan, and Sasha was going to clarify that.

"You just like Talan," she simply said.

"What?" Johnson replied, looking away from Talan, who now was listening to his iPod with his head tilted back, not watching.

"I know you liked Talan, but he's not—"

"I know, Sasha," Johnson snapped back, almost losing it. Someone's anger management classes aren't working. "The reason we don't hang out anymore is because it's over for you. The only reason guys talked to you was so that they could get with you. Girls liked you because you could bring the guys, but now it's done. You're not the leader for once anymore."

"I know, Johnson, but I'm happy. Congratulations on making the leader of the clique that used me. I hope you're happy." Sasha walked away. It finally hit Johnson. He wasn't happy.

Thirty minutes later and countless times overanxiously beating on the door, Lily found herself half-asleep . . . that was, until Talan approached her.

"Hey," he greeted her coolly as he sat down next to her at the very same spot she had sat down next to Johnson.

"Hey," she greeted him back, with a genuine smile on her face. She couldn't believe the boy she had been wishing she could talk to for so long was actually talking to her.

"So this is quite boring, huh?" he stated first.

"Yeah, it is," she said, not even able to look up from the wooden floor.

"You're dating that one kid, right?" he asked almost right after she finished *is*.

"Cliff?" she filled in.

"Yeah, him. Well . . ." He shifted and sat almost right in front of her. "When he talks to other people . . . do you ever get mad?" Is Talan Merrick actually asking Lily Carrington for dating advice?

"No."

"No?"

"Yeah."

"Ever?"

"If you really trust who you're dating, then you can't be controlling. Controlling relationships never endure," she made clear. Lily, as well as everyone else, knew that Talan wanted to control everything, so it was only natural that he wanted to control his relationship. We can see so much of his father in him already.

"Oh, okay. What does *endure* mean?" he asked in typical dumb jock style. Lily let out a small laugh.

"It means last. If you keep trying to control and be jealous of every person Sasha talks to, your relationship with her won't last. You can't be the only boy she is able to talk to."

"I know. She can talk to Johnson," he answered. Lily made an obvious face.

"Yeah, I know."

"Let's do a therapy session. I did one of these every week with my therapist in junior high."

Exactly fifteen minutes later, Talan approached Sasha and was ready to open up, except Sasha was about to stand up for herself.

"I'm 100 percent committed to this relationship, and you're not, Talan," Sasha declared. However, in romantic jock style Talan came up and hugged Sasha.

"My bad. It's just, I like you too much for you to be talking to other guys," he explained, taking away some things Shrink Lily had programmed into his brain. Sasha was speechless as Talan explained everything to her, all his problems.

Meanwhile, from a distance, Johnson crossly saw the duo make up, and as one pair crossed over and became closer, yet another drifted even farther apart. After they were done talking, Talan leaned in for a kiss, and just as his and Sasha's lips met, they heard a *click*.

"What is going on here?" Lydia asked as she stood by the doorway.

"Thank you so much!" Johnson cheered as he ran to the door. "They'll explain."

As the children made their way to their awaiting vehicles, they had thoughts about each other in their minds. As Talan glanced over at Lily getting into her SUV, he thought, *Thanks*, and gave her a cool smile. Lily looked back. She smiled, almost saying, *See, it does work*, and Talan grabbed Sasha's hand. Sasha watched as Johnson immediately got back on his phone and started texting. *I hope you have fun tonight*, was what she wanted to say to the rebellious heir, but as Johnson crossly met her eyes, he skipped over to Lily, and what she said haunted him, and his thought was basically, *Bitch*. Everyone has opinions and thoughts on other people. It's up to them to whether they secretly think the word, or actually say it. Until next time, it's *Miami Teen Social . . . .*

Chapter Nine

Thanksgiving Break

Thanksgiving break is a time for relaxation for the teens of Hamilton Prep, a time to escape the city, and go to Aspen or some wintry retreat for skiing, a romantic night out, clubbing, and/or of course salacious drama. It's the night of the last day of school before they can be released for their high-end vacations, and a football game is going on at Hamilton. They are playing none other than the Miami Catholic Prep School, big-time rivals. Talan is actually on the varsity team despite being a freshman (mhmm, wonder if Don had anything to do with that), but let's admit, he is pretty good at football. However, he was still upset he wasn't one of the starters.

All of the students were in the stands—in their respective cliques, of course—watching the game and cheering their little voice boxes out. That is, all except for Sasha, who was sitting with a bunch of people whom she didn't quite know. She had her hair neatly in a ponytail, and her friend beside her was the latest Marc Jacobs handbag. King bee, Johnson, was sitting a couple stands below, with, of course, his stingers at his sides—Emily and Lorraine. Jennifer was beside Emily, and all his little followers were dying to know what their king thought about the game. During time-outs, they sure did like to talk about Sasha. It was a varsity game, and the girls were only on the JV squad, so they weren't cheering.

The score was Hamilton 25, and MCP 22. The crowd was, to a certain extent, rowdy, and most of the conversations going on weren't about the game. Instead, they were about plans for Thanksgiving break.

"I can't wait to go back to Paris," Emily started. Good. Stay there.

"I'm going to New York City," Lorraine advised them. "Where are you going, Johnson?"

"I don't know," he replied pessimistically. He was thinking about what Lily had told him at cotillion practice. Did someone's words actually hit Johnson? Speaking of cotillion, it went by fantastically. Lily looked amazing in her dress, and the lily in her hair sure did the trick. Her newfound exquisiteness certainly got the very private senator's daughter some unwanted attention. Of course, Sasha stole the headlines with her jaw-dropping dress, which was an iridescent ivory, but in certain lights proved to be pink, a truly unconventional dress for cotillion, since it wasn't uncontaminated white.

During the last quarter of the game, something appalling happened. (It's not like it's the NFL. Hardly anything exciting happens in these games.) Talan was going out for a pass, and Riley Brooks, the star quarterback, spiraled the ball to him. Talan leapt up and caught it beautifully. Unfortunately, two seconds later he was tackled by two huge linebackers. Those Catholic school kids are somewhat meaty. The crowd flinched as they saw him go limp.

"That was fantastic." Emily smirked while adjusting the pearls on her neck. Lorraine giggled, and Johnson just rolled his eyes. Trouble in the beehive?

"Look at Sasha. Oh, she's crying," Emily teased as they all looked up at Sasha, who looked so troubled by her precious little boyfriend getting trampled. Sasha glanced down and saw them—their hateful faces. Tears started welling up in her perfect round eyes. God, when isn't this girl crying?

Just then, everyone saw as Johnson Sinclair walked out of the aisle and sat down next to none other than Sasha Chandler. Lily and Cliff, as well as the whole new school, knew that the power had been transferred within one of the most beautiful and powerful cliques in school, and Sasha was more confused than she was by the Burberry/Gucci sale when Johnson did that. Johnson simply held Sasha's hand as tears escaped from her eyes.

In the end, Talan ended up being okay. Big yay. Hamilton won, but the biggest talk was still about Johnson joining his ex-best friend, Sasha. People couldn't believe their eyes. What had happened that made Johnson do that? People were wondering. However, they were going to have to wait for answers.

Break provided an escape from the questions people had for Johnson, and up till now, an additional surprise was that Talan and Sasha were vacationing with Johnson at his lodge in Aspen, Colorado. The Sinclair home in Colorado was a cozy, welcoming four-bedroom, two-bath home valued at a warm million bucks. It was in the snowy mountain town, and was just an unforgettable place to be.

"This is amazing, Johnson," Sasha repeated as she walked around the large wooden oak living room with a huge window that covered a complete wall. The window exposed a small hill, with snow covering it and everything else.

"Thanks." Johnson directed his driver to put away the dozens of suitcases he brought for the one-week trip.

"This is really cool. Thanks for bringing us along," Talan thanked Johnson as he flopped on the couch. Johnson smiled and walked up the wooden stairs. Just then, Sasha followed him.

"Johnson," she called after him. He turned around. "I know we haven't really gotten the chance to talk, but this feels right . . . being with you," she said, nodding.

"I know," he agreed. "I couldn't be happier."

In the meantime, Lily Carrington decided to not go with her family on their annual trip to Aspen; she came down "sick" and had the whole mansion to herself, and of course the maids. Lily let them have Thanksgiving off. It looked as if Cliff couldn't afford a big, fancy vacation, and with more probing into Cliff Bowmen's history, we decided to write an article about him:

Despite looking like he comes from a railroad fortune, Cliff Bowmen, who escorted senator's daughter, Lily Carrington, to her recent cotillion, is actually not wealthy at all. He recently moved from Cheyenne, Wyoming, to Miami so he could attend Hamilton on a scholarship. Lily and Cliff, however, make it no secret that they are indeed an item at school, by kissing in public and holding hands. We have nicknamed the new couple, Liff. We wonder how the senator would feel if he knew that his daughter was dating a guy who probably couldn't even afford a Hermes bag for her. We also wonder if the new couple at Hamilton will create any rivalry for Talsha."

Comments-

SaraN_ says—Who cares if Cliff isn't rich. Lil is the only person at that school who is actually a good girl, and now she's found love. I have a friend who attends Hamilton and says that they're always together. Leave Lily alone and pick on the others. Poke fun at other kids who are way awful.

Adam/Eve_ says—I still can't believe that Johnson and Sasha aren't talking anymore. It's like Paris and Nicole. They have to be together!!! It's a truly sad day for their fans.

"What are you doing for Thanksgiving?" Cliff asked as he and Lily played croquet out in her spacious backyard, which seemed to go on and on. Lily shook the article out of her head that she had barely read from *Miami Teen Social* and threw her phone down on the spongy grass.

"I don't know. I was thinking that I was just going to go down and sleep on the beach," she advised him as she hit her ball. Cliff did a double take.

"What?" He was completely shocked. Was this the same Lily he knew? "Why?" he asked, laughing.

"My parents would never allow me to do it. Now that they're out of town, it seems like the perfect idea." She smiled. "I've always wanted to do something like that." Cliff was still skeptical as he hit his ball.

"Miss Lily, lunch is ready," Lorena, one of the maids, said as she approached the duo.

"Okay." Lily smiled as she hit her ball, and it went straight through one of the arches.

Even though it was sunny and warm in Miami, back in Aspen it was glittery with snow, and the temperature was frosty. Regardless of being told to take it easy on his ankle by his doctor, Talan was set on having a grand old time skiing. There he went, whizzing round and round down hills, and dodging pine trees.

"Maybe you should take it a little easier, Talan," Sasha suggested as he skidded to a sudden halt.

"Naw, this is the fun part, and besides, it's good for my ankle," he responded. The fashionable town of Aspen was packed with, of course, well-off families, but more important to Talan—beautiful young girls.

"I have an idea," Johnson added. "How about we have a race. We go all the way down this hill, and then finally stop at the coffee shop and get something to drink. Loser buys." Sure, like spotting for three cappuccinos is really something to fight for.

"Sounds like a plan," Sasha agreed as she adjusted her skis.

"Ready, set, go!" both Sasha and Johnson said as they took off. Talan was by far the better athlete, so he gave them a couple seconds' head start. How nice. Sasha was just naturally good at some sports (cheerleading and skiing being the only two), and Johnson had been skiing these very slopes since he was six. Talan took off, and it wasn't long until he wedged up next to Sasha.

"Hey, take it easy!" Sasha giggled through her goggles and cherry red scarf. Talan laughed as he passed her and quickly caught up with Johnson. He waved to Johnson as he passed him, and Johnson innocently flipped him the bird. Talan expressed his amusement as he cut him off and got in front of him. Talan was ahead of the pack, until a mysterious skier in a light blue jacket soon jammed in beside him.

"Dude!" Talan said as he almost lost his footing. The skier went faster, taking a different trail—with many pine trees. Not one to back down, Talan quickly followed the "dude" that almost made him fall. Soon, the dude and Talan were side by side. Talan pushed forward and exceeded the fellow. Just then, the mysterious guy came right next to Talan and pushed almost against him.

"What the hell! Get off me!" Talan looked up to see that he was being pushed to a side where a small snowy hill was just up ahead. Talan thought that if he were being forced to go up the hill, so was the guy that was pushing him. Just as Talan reached the hill, he snapped his pole on the inside of his competitor's ski, and they both raced off the hill, only to hurdle on a heavy mantle of snow.

"Why the hell did you push me?" Talan asked as he took off his face gear.

"Because you were challenging me," the "dude" replied as he took off his face gear. Talan was thunderstruck—not only was the dude a chick, but she was a gorgeous chick at that. She had long brown hair, and these savage disk-shaped hazel eyes.

"I'm Talan Merrick." Talan composed himself. The girl rolled her eyes.

"Ashley Levine," she replied.

"Where were you?" Sasha asked anxiously as Talan sauntered into the café. She glanced behind him to see that a girl—Ashley—was right behind him.

"Sorry, I accidentally took another trail, and went farther down the mountain," he informed her.

"Ashley, this is my girl . . . girlfriend, Sasha." He hesitated and then added, "And this is our friend, Johnson."

"Hi," Ashley greeted them in a cheery voice. She shook Sasha's hand, and Sasha was uneasy knowing that they had been together—alone. Talan and Ashley sat down at the table that was facing the window. The view engaged them with images of skiers skiing down mountains, truly a tranquil sight.

"So are you all from Miami?" Ashley asked as she drank a piping hot vanilla cappuccino.

"Yeah," Johnson answered, "and I didn't get where you were from."

"I'm from LA. I'm just here with my family for Thanksgiving break."

"Oh, I see," he replied. While Ashley talked, Sasha threw herself at Talan to make sure that Ashley recognized they were a very serious item. The rest of the day consisted of them getting to know their new friend, all the while cozying it up back at Johnson's lodge.

"This house is incredible, Johnson." Ashley walked around the whole house. "What the heck do your parents do? Work for the mob?" she joked. Maybe a possibility.

"No, my grandfather owns this real estate corporation back in Miami," Johnson responded.

"And I still can't believe that your dad is Don Merrick," Ashley said, not believing she had just run into football royalty, as she turned to Talan.

"Well, believe it," Sasha countered from Talan's side. Ashley almost flinched.

"What do your parents do?" Ashley asked the girl that seemed to be attacking her for every little comment she made. This didn't seem like sweet, dear Sasha.

"My stepfather is no longer here, but he was the head of a financial branch for a major Fortune Five Hundred company." Sasha got ominous, almost like the gray Aspen skies, talking about her stepfather. She remembered when he took her and her mom to Aspen a couple years ago—the memory itself was bittersweet.

"What do your parents do?" Sasha mimicked quite cruelly.

"Babe," Talan whispered.

"My dad owns a couple car dealerships," Ashley replied.

"There is this really hot band playing here tonight. We should all go," Johnson interjected.

"Sounds perfect," Ashley answered while looking at Sasha. Anyone smell a catfight a-brewing? "I should get going, though. My parents are probably wondering where I'm at, and I need to get ready. I think this clunky ski gear is making us look about ten pounds overweight," she added as she looked directly at Sasha.

"I'll show you out," Sasha responded. When Ashley left, Sasha of course became frenzied.

"Johnson, why did you invite her?" Sasha breathed, a little upset.

"What's wrong?" Talan asked soothingly. What? Talan actually caring about somebody that isn't himself?

"I was just being nice, and besides, I don't really want to be a third wheel to you and Talan," Johnson admitted.

"What third wheel? Johnson, we're like three peas in a pod." Sasha laughed. Johnson responded by laughing. After checking up with his guardian, which would be his lawyer, Johnson went up to the master bedroom, where a marvelous balcony met him. He walked out on it and lay on the edge, only to see Sasha and Talan out in the hot tub. Boy, Talan without a shirt, and low-riding trunks made Johnson's stomach ache. It would make anybody's stomach ache. Johnson had never had anybody to call his own. Sure, he had his chinchilla, and loads of friends, but he wanted someone—he wanted Talan. He knew that he couldn't get Talan like he got everybody else—with his money, of course, or even his social standing. He now comprehended (yes, for once in his life) that Sasha, his best friend, and Talan were dating, and he could see Talan as often as he wanted since he and Sasha were BFFs. Johnson was getting to the point in his life when he didn't care about friends. He wanted someone to feel affection for, to have a reason to get up in the morning. Johnson sighed before going back in the warmth of the lodge and changing into some darling Burberry partying clothes.

Ashley met the gang at a club in downtown Aspen, where the nightlife was almost as wild as that back in Miami. By the way, Ashley didn't look half-bad in a short black strapless Valentino dress. She had killer legs. The theme, one could say, that Johnson came up with was black and sexy. So, of course, he wore a black Burberry sweater with black slacks. Talan wore black slacks with a black button-up shirt. Sasha, who Johnson actually styled (Maybe after he runs his grandfather's business straight to the ground he can be a stylist. Who knows?), wore a sparkly Burberry mini with black tights, and to-die-for Prada stilettos.

"Ashley, you look beautiful," Johnson greeted Ashley with two warm kisses on the cheek. It somehow didn't sit well with Sasha.

"Thank you, and so do you. All of you," Ashley said, looking openly at Talan. "I can't believe you got us in here. I've been dying to get into one of these clubs for, like, forever now."

"Well, I guess we should have waited then, huh?" Sasha jokingly giggled about the "dying" part of Ashley's statement. There was a bit of tension in the room between the two girls as they all sat down in a booth. They all ordered drinks—alcoholic beverage, we might add—and soon started dancing. Talan and Sasha did what they always did on the dance floor and tried to have kids. Johnson was the life of the party and soon grabbed Ashley's hand and dragged her in and started to dance with her. The disco ball lit the room with a mixture of colors, and the DJ kept spinning the track, making for an overwhelming and unforgettable first night out.

"Hey, Johnson, I should really call my mom and check up on her," Sasha basically shouted into Johnson's ear a couple of hours later.

"Okay," he replied, nodding. Johnson ordered another drink from the bar and made his way up to his booth. As soon as he reached his destination, he became breathless. Ashley and Talan making out met his eyes. He blinked a dozen times before realizing that what he saw was authentic and not fake. He set his glass down and headed for the door.

He couldn't believe what Talan was doing. He was so stupid! As Johnson walked through a snowy alley without a jacket, he stopped. Talan wasn't his boyfriend, so why was he acting like he had just received a knife through his heart? He then finally grasped it. It was because he loved Sasha like a sister, and would do anything to look after her. Just then the sound of trash being emptied at a nearby restaurant broke up his thoughts,and Johnson wiped away tears that he didn't know were falling. Johnson could cry? Sinclairs had tear ducts?

"Are you okay?" a young man who seemed like he had just gotten off work asked Johnson. Johnson took a minute to evaluate him like he did every guy. The guy was cute . . . okay, really cute. He had short brown hair, and was well-developed in the muscle department. He was wearing the standard uniform of a fancy restaurant.

"Yeah," Johnson replied, "just a long night."

"Tell me about it," the guy replied. Johnson half-smiled, and soon a sudden familiar pain that hit him too often was back in his stomach. Was Talan around?

"Hi, I'm Johnson."

"Brendan." He reached out for Johnson's hand.

"So, do you live around here?" Brendan asked as he pulled out a smoke.

"No, I'm here for break. I live in Miami. What about you?" Johnson asked, interested.

"Unfortunately." He blew out a cloud of smoke. "Want one?" he asked.

"Sure." Johnson took one, and Brendan lit it for him. As soon it got lit, Johnson started choking on it.

"You don't smoke," Brendan said, smirking.

"I know," Johnson said as he threw the cigarette in the snow. "So, you work there?" Johnson asked as he looked at the restaurant.

"Yeah, my way out of this hell hole. Serving snobby rich people," he said, snorting.

"Know what you mean." Johnson tried to relate to the struggling gorgeous waiter.

"What?" Brendan replied, confused. "You said you were here on break. This is Aspen, man."

"Just because I'm here doesn't mean I'm rich," Johnson continued, still trying to connect.

"Sure," Brendan responded, not believing him. The two started to walk.

"So how old are you, Johnson?" Brendan suddenly asked. Johnson thought for a second. (Seems like Johnson is getting a lot of firsts this night. First understanding, and now thinking.) Brendan looked at least eighteen, and well, Johnson was fifteen.

"I'm seventeen," Johnson lied.

"Really? You look really young."

"How old are you?" Johnson asked.

"I'm nineteen." Johnson laughed and looked at Brendan the way you do when you like someone.

"You look like you're freezing. Here, have my jacket." Brendan slipped his jacket onto Johnson, and the two continued walking through the snowy town. They talked about everything and anything. Well, Johnson made up all lies. He said he was a junior this year at a public school in Miami, and his dad had skipped out on him, his mom, and sister (okay, that part was true), and his mom was a struggling painter. Then to his total chagrin, Brendan's history was almost identical. Jeez, wonder how guilty Johnson must have felt.

"That's crazy that both our dads skipped out on our families," Brendan repeated as he smoked another cigarette. Brendan's life story that he told was to say . . . more honest than the two-faced heir's. "I didn't know what I wanted to do after high school. I had a football scholarship, and I went to college, but I started drinking and experimenting with some drugs. My coach found out, I lost my scholarship, and I didn't have a way to pay for college, so I just dropped out," Brendan continued.

"Why did you move here?" Johnson asked.

"I dunno. One of my friends said it was a good party town," he said, smirking, "so I got a job at the restaurant and got an apartment, and that's that." Johnson's phone buzzed with a text.

Where are you??

It was from Sasha.

"Do you want to go back to my place?" Brendan asked out of the blue. Johnson took a deep breath.

"As much as I want to, and believe me I really want to, but I can't . . . my friend needs me."

"Okay, I understand." Brendan nodded.

"But I'll be here for a week." Johnson smiled, ending things on a sweet note. He kissed Brendan on his cheek before turning around and walking back to his lodge. Johnson was happy all the way back—honestly happy.

"Sasha," he called as he reached the lodge. He turned on the lights in the living room, and soon he saw Sasha outside through the window. She was standing on the hill. He went out the backdoor and called her name. Without the presence of Brendan around him, it seemed that the temperature had dropped fifteen degrees. He noticed he still had Brendan's jacket and smiled to himself.

"What are you doing out here? You'll catch your death, it's so freezing—" He stopped, seeing that Sasha was crying.

"Right over there"—Sasha pointed to a mountain a couple miles away past the town—"that's where my stepdad took my mom and me sledding."

"I'm sorry, Sasha." Johnson sympathized while he hugged his best friend.

"Sasha, you're my best friend, and I—" Johnson was about to tell her about how he saw Talan and Ashley kissing; however, abruptly Sasha would tell him something that would change everything, something she had been hiding. Her future would depend on what he would choose to do her secret. Johnson would hold her future to what he would choose to do with the secret.

"Hey, I've been looking for you." Talan came in and hugged Sasha. She and Johnson were sitting down on one of the couches, wrapped up in a quilt drinking hot chocolate, both their faces red with tears. "Dang, how long were you guys outside?" Talan asked as he poured himself a cup of chocolate and joined them. Johnson looked at Talan and noticed many things. One: Talan seemed exhausted even though it was still in the early hours of the morning. Two: Talan was missing his belt. Three: Talan was not the guy Johnson liked anymore.

Thanksgiving Day at the Carrington mansion was lonely. Lily had let all the maids, cooks, and housekeepers have the day off, something that her mother wouldn't ever have permitted. Lily was getting all her things ready for the beach; she packed a swimsuit, a sundress, a sun hat, sunglasses, flip-flops, and of course sunscreen. She strolled through her rather large sitting room, prancing around the marble floor, with a marvelous chandelier right above her. She had Mozart blasting though every room of the house. In the sitting room there were five huge wall-sized windows that let her see the humongous backyard. She sat at her black grand piano and played out her favorite piece by Beethoven, "Moonlight Sonata." She then quickly recognized how lonely her house was with just her, so she grabbed her bag and left. The only person she called was her driver, Davie, and he drove her to the beach. He was a little doubtful when she told him she was meeting with friends, since he knew that Lily liked to keep to herself. The sunny beach was almost dim when she arrived; the sky was a gray color and was overcrowding the sun.

"Guess I should have checked the weather." She kicked herself as she got her pale feet wet. It had been only about fifteen minutes when Lily concocted a genius plan in her head. She should go see Cliff. Even though Cliff had never told her where he lived, she didn't really find it odd. She called in some favors from one of her dear friends (a Hamilton Prep secretary) and found out where he lived. She called her driver and told him the location.

"Are you sure this is it?" Davie, her driver, asked.

"Huh." Lily looked around through her tinted SUV's window. The neighborhood was less than admirable. Lily didn't even know that places where people sat on the corners of streets passed out even existed. Then, to make matters worse, Lily had heard police sirens at least five times. She looked at the apartment and repeated the address a couple times to Davie.

"Yes, madam, this is the correct address," he guaranteed, even though he didn't even want her to roll down the window in fear they might get robbed.

"I'll call you later. Please pick me up here, Davie," she said, smiling.

"Miss, I don't really feel comfortable leaving you here. If your father found out . . ."

"Davie, it's okay. You know Cliff. I'll call you later." Lily stepped out of the SUV in nothing but a light orange sundress, flip-flops, and Chanel sunglasses. She walked up to the apartment.

"Carl sucks . . . ugh! How horrible!" Lily was revolted as she read some graffiti on the side of the apartment. She swiftly, but neatly, went up the stairs and found Cliff's door number. "This is it," she said, and smiled. She noticed her hand was shaking. She knew it wasn't polite etiquette, going to someone's house unannounced, and especially on a holiday, but she wanted to wish Cliff a happy Thanksgiving. She then knocked on the door gracefully.

"Lily!" Cliff sounded more shocked than happy when he answered the door. He closed the door behind him. "What are you doing here?"

"I came to see you and wish you a happy Thanksgiving," Lily answered, almost wishing she hadn't come, since it now seemed like a bad idea.

"You should have called me first. I mean, this is only a temporary place," he explained, obviously stressed out from her sudden company.

"What's wrong?" Lily asked.

"I just . . . I didn't want you to see where I lived," he admitted, finally caving in.

"I don't care where you live—"

"You bitch, where's my money!" they heard someone yell from the bottom floor of the apartments.

"Come on," Cliff said as he took Lily into the "safety" of the apartment. Lily had never seen anything like Cliff's apartment before. It was small—smaller than her bedroom. She could see the living room and the kitchen/dining room all from where she was standing.

"Cliff, who was it, sweetie?" Cliff's mom asked as she peered out from the kitchen.

"It's Lily." Cliff sounded like it was his and Lily's first date, he was so tense.

"Oh!" Cliff's mom, Susan, basically came running from the kitchen. She had curlers in her hair and was wearing an apron. "It's such an honor to meet you, Miss Carrington," Susan gasped. Lily giggled.

"Thank you. I love your place, and please call me Lily." Lily now felt like it was the right thing to do, coming to Cliff's home.

"I wish Cliff would have told me you were coming; this place is a mess," she apologized, looking around the living room.

"No, it's fine," Lily said, smiling.

"Will you be joining us for Thanksgiving?" Susan asked with an expression on her face like she had won the lottery.

"If it's okay with you, I would be more than happy to," she answered. Lily held Cliff's hand. Susan smiled disbelievingly.

"Is it okay with your parents . . . the senator?" she asked, almost breathless.

"They're out of town," she answered.

"I'm so happy." Susan sat Lily down on the couch.

"Do you mind," Lily interrupted politely before Susan could get another word in, "if I help with dinner?"

"Why, absolutely, you can help." She softly grabbed Lily's hand and led her to the kitchen. "Now . . . oh, where is it? Oh, here it is. This is my favorite stuffing recipe. It's quite simple . . ." She started explaining how to make it. Lily looked up to see Cliff leaning against the arch of the small kitchen, smiling. She smiled back, thinking—she wished this was her life.

After cooks spent hours arranging a lovely meal, it was spent with only Talan enjoying it. Ashley had Thanksgiving with her family, Johnson spent the day in his room, feeling plagued with responsibility and guilt, and Sasha was right by Talan's side, except Sasha felt thankful that she had let her secrets out. She believed she had been let out of a cage that had trapped some part of her, but unknown to her, she had transferred her old feelings to the one person she trusted and confided her secrets to.

"Brendan," Johnson said as he saw the man he wished he could have gotten to know more at the restaurant. It was the last day of break, and Johnson had been caged up in the pleasing-to-the-eye master bedroom watching TV and drinking wine. "I'm really sorry I haven't come by and talked to you."

"Yeah, so am I. I'm really busy. I don't have time for games," Brendan made clear as he cleared a table. "Lunch for one?"

"Brendan, please. I feel so bad. It's just . . . you have no idea what I have been dealing with these last couple of days—"

"Brendan, get back to work," the manager of the restaurant ordered.

"I have to go."

"Here." Johnson ended the conversation as he handed Brendan an envelope. "It's a check for almost ten thousand dollars. Go back to school, Brendan. Good-bye." Johnson kissed Brendan on the cheek once before exiting the restaurant. He wanted to leave already. He felt like he was going to crumple away if he spent another second in Aspen, but he knew that he had to help Brendan first.

All the way back to Miami, Johnson wept in secret. He cried for himself, he cried for Brendan—but most of all he cried for Sasha, and the horrible thing she did.

Thanksgiving break for most kids is a time for them to relax and spend time with their families. For Hamilton Prep kids, it's a time for secrets and heartbreak. What the future holds for Sasha and Talan is undefined. Will the opportunity for a mate be brought back up for Johnson? Who knows? And will Lily learn to love the life she was born with, despite her having everything anybody could possibly want? This is *Miami Teen Social.* Happy Holidays.

Chapter Ten

Bonfire

Almost as soon as school came back in, it's gone almost like last year's Gucci. Two weeks have gone by, and yet it is time for another break . . . Christmas break. Instead of wintry getaways, Christmas is the time for some fun in the sun. Cabo San Lucas, Cancún, or some other exotic resort in Mexico is usually the destination for these out-of-control twits.

The freshman class decided to have a little get-together bonfire on the beach after school—a time for friendly mingling, juicy gossip, and of course interesting drama. All organized by class president Lily Carrington.

"Are you looking forward to the bonfire tonight?" Emily asked Johnson as they sat in the lounge at Hamilton together.

"Yeah, are you?" Lorraine asked before he could even answer.

"I dunno," Johnson replied blandly.

"What's wrong?" Jennifer chipped in, detecting his tone. "These last two weeks you've been acting totally exhausted and run-down." Jennifer sat on the edge of the couch, concerned about her friend.

"Are you doing cocaine?" Lorraine solicited.

"No, Lorraine, I'm not taking drugs," Johnson retorted as he got up and walked out of the lounge. Lorraine is a little blunt, isn't she?

"He totally is," his second "best friend" Emily alleged. "Look at this article on *Miami Teen Social*." She read it aloud.

> Since Thanksgiving break has been done with, wild child heir Johnson Sinclair also seems to be. Rumors from inside sources say that the heir is roaming around Hamilton like

a zombie. Drugs, anyone? Ever since he and gal pal Sasha Chandler, and her boy toy Talan Merrick took a trip to Johnson's Aspen lodge, he has just been out of sorts. It is also reported that he had a fling with a waiter who worked at Cecile's, a high-end restaurant there in Aspen, but maybe breaking things off was just too much for the poor boy, so he turned to coke to cope. Such a shame, *not!* He was headed down the route anyway, such a familiar route maybe 'cause his father took the same one.

Comments~

miamihottiegurl says—Johnson Sinclair and Sasha Chandler need to dig a hole and bury themselves in it, and then Talan could dig a hole right next to them and bury himself in that one! They are all pathetic losers!!

bobbyjojo says—it's a low blow to bring his father into this. And I heard Johnson was doing quite well. However, I seriously doubt that he is doing drugs. He's never out anymore, and cokeheads are out till all hours of the night. I haven't seen him party once in these last couple weeks. I can only imagine what his lawyer is thinking, since she has to report his status back to the judge every month. Something tells me she will not be happy to hear that there are drug rumors circulating about him.

"What's been up with Johnson lately?" Faiday Hayward questioned Sasha and Talan as he messed with his newly installed lip ring. Emily said he would look quote/unquote "sexy" with one, and they're not even dating really, but he still got one.

"I dunno. He seems normal to me," Talan replied while kissing Sasha's neck. Nowadays, Talan's favorite thing to do has been to nibble on Sasha's neck, and she did a low side ponytail just for the occasion. Sasha just giggled as Talan lightly bit into her.

"Have you noticed Johnson?" Lily almost mimicked Faiday to Cliff while Johnson walked past them . . . well, more like shuffled. Poor little cokehead couldn't even keep his feet up.

"Yeah, yesterday in science, he slept through the entire class, and usually, he never wants to shut up," Cliff informed her. Lily splintered a smile, but soon she grew upset about Johnson. Everybody was saying he was on drugs, and what she told him at cotillion practice loomed every now and then in her head.

So it looked as if everyone was talking about the famous, rebellious heir doing drugs. Truth be known, the only drug Johnson was overdosing on was depression mixed with a spoonful of guilt. Sorry, Johnson haters, but not any cocaine for him, at least that we know of . . . and we know everything.

The bonfire that night was on full blast. Beer was in a chilled tub, cigarettes were on hand, and everyone who was anybody managed to show up. These bonfires, however, just more often than not have their own little cliques within the whole class. Lily and Cliff stood among the other future scientists and doctors, and even perhaps some senators were among them. They, nonetheless, were not the geeky crowd, with their millionaire scientist parents who invented God knows what. They stood there texting on their up-to-the-minute cell phones that had barely come out an hour ago, or listening to fourth-generation iPods that wouldn't be available to the public for three months. Lily showed up wearing a plaid skirt more or less bordering on the likes of a naughty schoolgirl outfit. Her top consisted of a V-neck sweater with an undershirt. She gave the impression of being totally preppy in that getup. That crowd talked mainly about what a beautiful night it was, and what relatives they were going to visit for Christmas break. Everyone was extremely curious about the senator's daughter's answers. Maybe she'll become the queen termite of that group.

The prep/jocks were in another crowd. Tonight—miracle of miracles—they managed to put the entire exasperating catfighting aside. Faiday, Talan, and a couple of their other self-absorbed footballer friends stood amongst the pretty girls, and of course Johnson made an appearance. (It took loads of convincing from Sasha and Emily to get him there.) Sasha and Jennifer seemed to be carrying on a conversation. It seemed like the only person Sasha carried a sentence with lately was Talan, and that was just borderline. Emily and Faiday's on again/off again fling was back on as they made out. Guessing the lip ring worked. Lorraine managed to flirt with three boys all at the same time, and it looked as if they weren't even aware that she was flirting with the others. Now, those are skills a future stripper should know. Good job, Lorraine! Johnson was remote in his psyche, as he always was lately.

"Want a smoke, Johnson?" Emily inquired as she took a puff of a cigarette.

"God, I do," Lorraine answered, grabbing one and quickly lighting it. All the guys soon took out beers and started to drink, and as alcohol and nicotine surged though their systems, music almost immediately bellowed from fancy Escalades. They were all enjoying themselves, having fun drinking and smoking, and hanging out with their boyfriends or girlfriends. Even Lily was dancing with Cliff on the pliable sand having fun. If Lily could have fun and let loose, anyone could. The time flew by like the beers did out of the coolers.

Johnson found himself face-to-face with the boundless, shadowy ocean at one point in the night. He slowly started to stride through the icy, salty water. It felt better, he decided, to feel the same way on the outside as he did on the inside, frozen and infinite.

"Johnson"—Sasha was behind him on the edge of the beach—"what are you doing?" Johnson looked down and was waist deep in water. "Johnson," he heard Sasha say once more. He dove deep down and submerged himself in cold water.

"Johnson." Johnson looked up to see his therapist, Julie Kimp, talking. He was in a session in her office in Brickell. They were on the fifteenth floor, and he could see out the window and observe other massive structures. The office he was in was pale; it was filled with light olives, off-whites, and a lot of crystals. "You have to say something, Johnson. You've been seeing me for the past week and a half, and we're still on step one." Johnson took a deep breath.

"My friend told me something," he finally made clear.

"Like what?"

"Something."

"You don't have to say anything you don't want to, Johnson, but remember this is strictly confidential," she assured him with a warm smile.

"What she told me is bothering me." Johnson felt uncomfortable again. He felt bizarre. He had said so little, but she had said so much, and every time he wanted to say something, he got the feeling that he shouldn't, that he should protect his friend and keep her secrets.

"Why is it bothering you?" she asked. Johnson believed that's all she did; ask why, and ask.

"She's my best friend. We've been best friends since I can remember, and she confided something in me, but I don't know if I can . . ." He stopped. Julie knew the Sinclairs really well; after all, she was their therapist. She waited a couple seconds to say something.

"On a good note, school is half over with, and Christmas break is here," she said, trying to cheer up the depressed kid. "Do you have any plans for break?"

"My best friends and their boyfriends are going to Cabo in a couple days," he answered.

"Are you going?"

"I don't want to."

"Johnson," Julie said sternly, "you're young. You need to enjoy yourself. You have been doing wonders with your anger management. I talked to Berna, and she said you should be done with those sessions before the New

Year starts. Have fun this Christmas break, Johnson. If fact, I think I'm going to prescribe you something that I think will help," she confirmed with an affectionate smile. Getting some happy pills perhaps?

Ciao, fellow readers, because even for being gossips we still need our breaks. Rest up, read a lot, and don't party too hard. Will Christmas break have an effect on any of our Hamilton kids? Will they embrace the good old holiday spirit, or what will happen when you take all those kids and put them in a giant house in Mexico? Will the beautiful sea (which is way better than the one in Miami), the calming sand, and the thrilling Mexican nightlife be more than enough to keep these twits happy, or will drama ruin the holiday? Of course it will. Talan with all those girls; it would be a miracle if one doesn't end up preggers. Will some Prozac truly brighten up gloomy Johnson? What will he do during break? It's *Miami Teen Social*. Happy Holidays, everyone.

Chapter Eleven

Vacation Is Over

Welcome back, everyone! We hope you had a fantastic Christmas and New Year's, and also anticipate that you have set high resolutions and expectations for yourselves for the new year (something tells us that our Hamilton Prep kids have not even thought about wasting brain cells thinking about resolutions and such, but then again they always surprise us). Boy, so much has happened in a matter of weeks. One thing stayed the same, however; Talan being faithful to his girlfriend of five months was not on his resolution list. While on vacation with his friends and girlfriend, Sasha Chandler, in Mexico it is reported that he linked up with the owner of the beach house (and Sasha's friend), Lorraine Everly. Reportedly, Sasha was asleep on the couch after a long night of partying when the affair happened. We only wonder what Sasha will believe.

"God, I'm so tired," Sasha told Talan as she lay against him as they walked back to Lorraine's beach house. They were walking along the dark streets of Cabo (let's only hope that they do not get mugged); it was an unnatural setting for the Hamilton Prep kids, who were used to golden roads and gated houses. Instead, here in Cabo, the only gated things were prisons.

"Once we get to back to the house, you can sleep." Talan kissed Sasha on her forehead. The pair were both wearing bathing suits and flip-flops; that's all they wore on their little trip. They were also equally very smashed from fruity Mexican drinks and beer. And for the cherry on top of the ice cream, once they reached the house, they struggled to get inside; Talan was howling loudly and Sasha was giggling, making their neighbors who were trying to sleep (you know, since that's what most decent people do at three in the morning) think that a burglary was going on. The house was less than what any parent would want to see. Bathing suits and trunks were left on $3,000 Dior party dresses, $700 Prada stilettos were crowded on the stairs leading up to the rooms, and $2 plastic dishes and cups were cockeyed in the sink.

"Where's the damn maid?" Talan questioned as he kicked rags that were in his way.

"How was the beach party?" Lorraine asked as she came down the stairs in a bathing suit with some pink dotted Burberry pumps. (Who does that?) Another thing that their parents probably wouldn't be fond of was their partying every night. Of course the rest of the gang—Emily, Faiday, and Jennifer—were still on the beach partying away like there was no tomorrow. At this appalling scene one might ask, why the heck are their parents letting them run wild in another country!? Well, to answer that, these deceitful preps all have ready-made answers, such as, "Oh, blank's handlers are chauffeuring us," which are completely fabricated. The only chauffeurs are maids and drivers who bend over backward to do what they want.

"It was all right," Talan reported as he walked a tipsy Sasha, whose blond hair was tangled to the back of her sticky neck, a far snivel from the lovely Sasha most know. He laid her down, and she promptly slumbered away like a newborn baby.

"Gosh, she's totally wasted," Lorraine informed Talan as she walked over and laid her head on his shoulder.

"Yeah." Talan smirked. Lorraine managed to let out a little moan and put her arm around Talan's waist. He looked up, and quicker than Lorraine could seize up the hottest Chanel bag, his lips were uncontrollably on hers. They made out like wild pigs did in Africa. Since Lorraine was such a good friend, she decided to take Talan up to her room, where Sasha couldn't witness anything, despite sleeping like she was in a coma. It looked like it was going to be another remarkable night for Talan, scoring with not only one, but two girls. Just then, another beautiful girl would put a damper on it.

"Jennifer!" Lorraine yelped as Jennifer stood at the doorway, with her striking black hair draping down the front of her. Jennifer looked somewhat disenchanted by Talan, who always had made her swoon. Sasha groaned from the couch.

"Let's go to sleep, Sasha," Talan broke in as he quickly went to the couch and got Sasha and took her upstairs. The whole time, Jennifer hung about at the doorway, coming across as if her boyfriend had moved all over again. That's the kind of friend you want to surround yourself with. If she decides to tell, it's anybody's guess. Later, she would call Johnson to see what she should do.

Johnson Sinclair spent his Christmas break in Miami. His Prozac surely did help, and the once-depressed boy, who was now all smiles, had day-by-day plans for break. After coming home at around three, four, five in morning, he would sleep until three in the afternoon and get ready for the night, and the cycle would repeat. Now, instead of a zombie, he was like a vampire. The nightclub and friends were different, but a variable that remained constant was that he would take his Prozac every night before leaving. Best of all, despite having a court order to stay away from Frizzy Lizzy Van Ryan, he was seen on more than one occasion partying it up with her.

"I'm so glad we're friends again," Frizzy Lizzy told the heir as they danced in neon rocked-out, Set Miami.

"Yeah, me too. Your life isn't the same without a religious slut in it," he gagged. Lizzy threw her head back, hysterically laughing. It really wasn't that funny. Frizzy was wearing a dank Hawaiian-inspired tie-dye dress by some London designer. Johnson was wearing the typical refined Ralph Lauren look. Johnson reached down in his coat pocket and hugged the bottle of Prozac with his hand. God, how he loved those little pills. They had truly made a remarkable turnaround for him.

Lily Carrington told yet another lie to her parents when they took a trip to our dear country's capital, Washington, DC. It was more business than anything, so they let her stay home—again. And Lily had the most important event happen to her over the break. A thing that all teenagers brag about—the loss of her good old V card.

"Okay," Cliff concluded as he finished kissing Lily in her bedroom.

"What?" Lily said, caught off guard all hot and full of endorphins.

"This is usually how far we take it," Cliff reminded her. What guy stops when they're not told to? Oh, a gentleman, of course, such as Cliff Bowmen.

"Well, I don't think we should stop," she made known. Wow, who would have known Lily was such a little savage?

"Really?" he asked.

"Yeah . . . I know virginity is such a sacred value for a young lady, but I don't think you should wait for marriage, because I'm young and I want to experience life, and if I die tomorrow I don't want to die not experiencing the one thing almost every kid in school does every night. Granted, some people take advantage of it, and horrible things happen to them—pregnancy and STDs—but if we're careful, then it's fine. Have you ever done it before?" she rambled for what seemed like hours.

"No."

"Okay," she said, smiling. She resumed kissing him, and Cliff made his way down to her blouse.

"Wait!" Lily interrupted.

"What?" Cliff said, panicked like he had crossed the line.

"Can we go to your house?" she breathed. "I feel so much more comfortable there than I do here." What? The senator's daughter feels more at ease at a cramped apartment located where people sell crack than at her mansion, where people sell, well . . . people?

"Sure," Cliff replied, nodding. So after a quick drive from good old Davie to Cliff's apartment, they were back where they left off but in a new setting.

"I love you," Lily made clear before anything else happened.

"I love you, too," Cliff confirmed as he kissed Lily's soft lips.

Was it worth it—Lily waiting? Sasha and Talan waited—let's see—a couple days after they were dating to experience sexual intercourse, and Lily and Cliff waited four months. But was it also worth it for Lily to skip out on meeting the president to lose her V-card? Well, the next day she spent the whole afternoon in bed rolling around complaining that she didn't feel good. Those first days after your first time are sure brutal, though, but it seems worth it.

With articles out about their little vacation, the clique that enclosed Sasha, Talan, Emily, Faiday, Lorraine, and Jennifer seemed tighter than ever (maybe because they were all sleeping with one another). They pranced around school that January with couples hand in hand, and Lorraine thinking she ruled the school because the most exciting thing that happened over break had managed to occur at her place in Mexico. They couldn't care less about the cheating scandal, even though everyone was thinking about it. It did irritate Sasha's mind, about it getting out and everyone finding out. If someone comes to the magazine with such a scandal, we can't help but to publish it, and all they want in return is a little exposure. Soon, the clique splintered off as if everyone watching them weren't good enough. Talan and Faiday went to their weight-lifting class, where they were treated like gods amongst the other jocks. The girls—well, the girls had drama to cause as always.

"Johnson"—Sasha smiled as she saw her best friend, who was absent from the clique, sitting on the edge of one of the big windows on the stairs—"why haven't you called us?" She laughed as she sat next to him. The heir was looking out the window and into the sunny sky, Dolce & Gabbana sunglasses shielding his eyes from the powerful rays.

"I was busy," he replied. Sasha and Jennifer looked at each other, confused.

"Yeah, hanging out with Frizzy Lizzy. We read about that. What's up with that?" Jennifer asked as she shifted her weight on her five-inch platform heels.

"I dunno," he said, shrugging.

"We had a blast in Mexico. You should've come," Sasha said, trying to comfort her friend, who seemed depressed again. Jeez, run out of Prozac?

"I know. I read about it." He smirked back as he turned around and took off his sunglasses. Jennifer and Sasha, without a sound, struggled for breath. Johnson looked totally washed up again. His hair was messy, and his eyes were bloodshot. He saw the look on their faces.

"Sorry . . . it's just . . . I ran out of Prozac—Yay! We were right—"and I totally feel like Kirstie Alley. All fat and ineffective." He tried to smile.

"You're on Prozac?!" Jennifer almost shrieked. Johnson got up and hushed her.

"Yes," Johnson whispered, "and I don't want anyone to find out." He looked at Sasha, and she looked down, knowing why he was on antidepressants. Dr. Kimp, make room in your schedule for another depressed Hamilton Prep kid.

Lorraine and Emily clacked down the hallway to the class president and her boyfriend. Wonder what's going to happen.

"Hey, Cliff," Lorraine simpered.

"Hey, Lorr . . . Lorraine," Cliff stumbled. Lorraine looked at Emily and giggled.

"Isn't he so cute?" she told Emily. Lily stood behind Cliff and moved her eyes to the floor.

"Hi, Lily," Lorraine said, smirking. Lily smiled, trying to look like the welcoming class president she was.

"So there's this party tomorrow night at Talan's, and you should come," Lorraine kindly informed Cliff as she set her hand on his shoulder.

"I'll see," Cliff replied, blushing. Lily almost choked, and she walked away in her black stilettos. Lorraine and Emily looked at each other, amused.

"See you there." Lorraine hugged Cliff as she saw Lily turn around. Cliff remained stiff as a board. After what seemed like five minutes of hugging, Emily and Lorraine walked away, and in next to no time turned around as they took notice of Lily and Cliff arguing. Jeez, corrupting one relationship wasn't enough for little Miss Lorraine, was it? Now she has to go for another one.

"Oh, my God! Lily, get Cliff. I'm drowning!" Lorraine chatted as she pretended to drown at the start of swimming class when Lily walked in. (Oh *my* God, if you hear our cries, do please drown her, God.) Lily tried to contain herself and strolled off to the locker room.

"Stupid whore," Lorraine mouthed as she swam in circles with her follower Hannah Reynolds—who, pointless to say, was despised by king bee Johnson for dating a guy he liked—trailing right behind her. Wonder what the punishment is for hanging around someone who Johnson hates? He's out of antidepressants, so he's moodier then a sales clerk at a Saks during a fashion sale.

Because of Coach Williams's hard workout to-do list, Lily had practically evaded Miss Lorraine and her ruthless, defiant stare, but that was not for long, and in the locker room, they finally came head-to-head. As Lorraine changed out of the standard blue one-piece bathing suit and changed into her school uniform, she made some comments.

"I have such an amazing rack. Cliff stares at it all day." She smirked as she buttoned up her shirt, and purposely left a couple buttons unfastened. "Isn't that right, Lily?" She turned to Lily, who was rolling up her tights getting ready to slip on her Pradas.

"What is your problem, Lorraine?" Lily finally asked, summing up the courage. Girl fight?

"Excuse me?" Lorraine snapped as she stepped up to Lily. All the girls gathered around to see the class bitch and the class president argue.

"Cliff is my boyfriend, and you should respect that," Lily said, with her voice obviously trembling with fear. All the girls surrounding them closed in.

"Are you going to make me respect it?" Lorraine growled. Lily took a deep breath.

"You've already ruined one relationship. Stop being such a wrecker. It's not a good look." It took only those words for Lily to walk away, and it took only those words for Lorraine to yell and grab Lily's dark hair. It basically ended with the other girls pulling them apart. It wasn't much of a fight, but for Hamilton it was first-class news.

"You bitch. I hate you!" Lorraine yelled as the girls took her out of the locker room. Of course all the girls gathered around their president and helped comfort her skull, which was tender. Poor Lily, sad face.

So vacation is definitely over. Drama never left and probably never will. The day was started with conversations about the love triangle that happened in Mexico, and the day ended with conversations about Lily Carrington and Lorraine Everly getting into a scuffle over a boy from Wyoming. Obviously, these kids haven't set high expectations for themselves, but hey, they sure are compelling. This is *Miami Teen Social*, signing off.

Chapter Twelve

Fights, Love, and Fights

Fights, love, and fights are the most gripping things to talk about. Everyone loves a good catfight, and everyone loves seeing some love. Better believe that there is going to be plenty of fight and love in store as the school year goes on.

"I have something for you," Talan told Sasha as they lay in his bedroom.

"What it is?" Sasha asked, sounding like a baby. Even though she hated to say it, all Sasha could think about was the article on *Miami Teen Social* about Lorraine and Talan. It had been a while, but she was so disgusted at herself that she was too tired to realize Talan needed someone there for him. Talan pulled out a ring. Oh my, what's this? Sasha gasped, surprised.

"It's a promise ring," he said, smiling. Who on Earth knew that Talan was so romantic! What is going on? Maybe Talan felt guilty . . . nah, he definitely didn't. Sasha fumbled with the ring in her clumsy little hands, and Talan took over with his controlling hands and put it on her ring finger. The ring was a small pink diamond on a silver band. It was actually quite adorable.

"Talan, I love it!" Sasha applauded as she kissed her boyfriend fervently on the lips. Talan kissed back, and with one hand grabbed on to her head and with the other started to take of his T-shirt—gosh, multi-tasking much?? After Talan took off his shirt, he slipped off something of Sasha's and then he took off his shorts. He went back to Sasha, and it doesn't take rocket science to figure out what was going on. He then made a trip to his nightstand and retrieved the most bragged-about thing in a young male teenager's nightstand—obviously the reason why Sasha wasn't pregnant yet. And that's how the cookie crumbled. Guess the ring was just a lay present.

"I'll text you later. I'm going to the gym," Talan told Sasha as he finished taking a shower.

"It's almost seven," Sasha replied as she fixed herself up, including adjusting her new ring.

"Faiday, Ashton, and a couple of the other guys are all going. So I decided to go too."

"Oh," Sasha answered back. "I guess I could go shopping with Johnson." Talan smiled, knowing he was the only guy she should be hanging with.

"Love you." Sasha beamed as Talan got his gym bag and headed out of his room.

"Okay, see you later," Talan confirmed.

"Isn't it beautiful?" Sasha bragged as she and Johnson strolled along Sunset Place at seven thirty in the evening, drinking double chocolate chip Frappuccinos and shopping.

"Yeah, it is," Johnson answered for the fiftieth time. The two were walking with Johnson's handlers right behind him. They were telling Berna on the phone (aka Johnson's lawyer, and the only person who actually watched him besides those crazy chaperones, who always seemed to be lacking judgment) what Johnson's status was. Berna had been on overtime keeping a close eye on Johnson, like he was on suicide watch, which for her was the case. Johnson and Sasha also had managed to rack up an impressive tab for their little shopping trip, which Sasha had paid for. She still sensed he was depressed, and all she thought about was his being on Prozac. She wanted to talk about it, but she felt like it was talking about rape to a rape victim. It just didn't fit well.

While heading out of Sunset Place, they managed to run into none other than Jace Costillo, who Sasha hadn't talked to since the cotillion, since that caused a huge fight between her and Talan. She couldn't help but say hi.

"Hi, Jace," Sasha him greeted warmly as she gave him a hug.

"Hello, Sasha," he said sarcastically, like he hadn't seen her in ages. Jace was a lot taller than Sasha, even though she was rail thin and pretty tall for her weight of around one hundred pounds. He still had his crutches and foot brace on.

"This is my best friend, Johnson," Sasha introduced them in her infantile voice, which was, in fact, quite annoying.

"Yeah, I know. I think you went to my cousin Justin's party a while back, right?" he asked, very welcoming.

"Yeah, I guess," Johnson responded, staring off into space.

"All right, you're the talkative type," Jace joked. Sasha innocently giggled and shook her head.

"So, what are you doing here?" Sasha asked, beaming with a cute smile spread across her tan face. Is there a guy that Sasha doesn't glow around?

"Nothing much. Just here with some of the guys hanging around. What about you?"

"Just here with Johnson shopping."

"I can see that." Jace looked behind them to see two brawny guys in suits carrying a bunch of shopping bags. Sasha out of the blue jumped up and grabbed Jace's white hat, almost making him fall.

"Hey!" He laughed as he grabbed her small wrists and tried to grab his hat back. Johnson rolled his eyes at the flirtatious pair. "So what's your number?" Jace soon asked. Sasha gulped. What? Was Sasha Chandler going to give out her number to another guy? Well, we're going to have to wait a staggering two seconds to find out. She reached into Jace's pocket and pulled out his phone, and added in her digits.

"We should get going," Sasha concluded as she handed Jace back his phone. For just a split second, their hands grazed as she offered him his phone back.

"'Bye." Jace drooled as he looked at Sasha as she and Johnson walked away. Sasha leaned into Johnson and started to giggle. If Johnson hadn't been so depressed, he probably would have tried to make everything about him. Sasha decided that she hated that her best friend felt depressed, and tonight was the only night she would let herself feel all right that he was depressed. She needed a moment to think about the predicament she was in.

If Sasha thought that Johnson being depressed was coming to an end, she was sorely mistaken. The next day at school, an article from yours truly, *Miami Teen Social*, would have the whole school buzzing.

> Spending tons of cash on clothes, doing drugs, and partying every night seems to be the appropriate mix for depression—at least for Miami heir and Hamilton Prep student Johnson Sinclair. Sources are now claiming that the heir is in fact on Prozac. For all of those who don't know what Prozac is, it's depression medication. With all his nonstop partying with Frizzy Lizzy and her Catholic gang over break, it's a surprise the poor kid didn't OD. Too bad, huh?
>
> Comments~
>
> K!KI says—I know I've made fun of Johnson a lot, but I feel bad that he's all depressed. I guess he's taking the breakup from what's his name from Aspen really bad. Does anyone know who that guy is? I'm dying to know!!
>
> Adam/Eve says—The guy's name is Brendan McKenzie, and he's just a waiter. My cousin lives in Aspen and knows him. I guess he's a really big partier. That combination wouldn't have worked, because Johnson needs to slow down. And what happened to his grandpa threatening to cut him off if he didn't stop partying??

Johnson felt like all eyes were watching him like he was some rare animal at the zoo. Berna had tried to do everything to take down the "absurd and false" claims that *Miami Teen Social* had posted about her client, so it went down, but not before each person at Hamilton read it. Mission accomplished.

"It's okay, Johnson," Sasha soothed Johnson during lunch.

"I just don't know how people found out about this. It's for medical purposes. Isn't there a confidential block that stops people from finding out about these things?" Johnson cried. Yes, cried.

"Whoever leaked it, Johnson, is probably more heartbroken and miserable than you," Lorraine said, "trying" to calm him. Johnson looked at her, bemused. "Doesn't it have to do with Brendan from Aspen?" she asked quietly. Guess she also read the article. Johnson pouted even more.

"Here, have some of my green tea," Jennifer offered. All the girls did their best to console Johnson.

"If it helps any, I take protein shakes," Faiday said. They all stared at him for a moment. "They help me build muscle mass, and Prozac helps him be . . . not so depressed. What's the difference?"

"Let's go get Johnson a water." Emily dragged Faiday from the table and scolded him as they walked away.

"What? I thought I was helping!" Faiday declared.

"Maybe you should try talking to Berna," Sasha suggested.

"Or going back to the therapist," Jennifer put in. They both looked at Talan to see if he had any ideas. He had his hands folded on the table and was using it as a headrest and was dozing off. Sasha cleared her throat, and his eyes, without delay, shot open.

"Huh? Maybe you should try talking to your mom." He cleared his throat. Sasha and Jennifer, both knowing the relationship (or lack of) between Johnson and his mother, rolled their eyes.

"You know . . ." Johnson finally spoke, "I think I'll do that."

"Hi, Cliff," Lorraine and Emily teased as they walked by him and Lily. Lily responded by kissing Cliff in a rather sensual display of PDA. Raising the bar perhaps?

"I think we should go to that party at Talan's," Cliff proposed as soon as Lily finished kissing him.

"I wish we could. But I have a cello recital I have to practice for, and my mom is also making me practice piano tonight. Not to mention, we have to study for the algebra quiz tomorrow," she reminded him.

"Oh," Cliff said, sounding like he would rather attend the party, and Lily noticed.

"But maybe after we finish that, we could watch a movie, or catch up on the news." Was Lily for real? Unless she was offering another round of intercourse with that news pitch, maybe Cliff wouldn't join her for the night.

"We'll see," Cliff ended as they both walked off to class hand in hand.

As his driver pulled up to Johnson's massive gated home, Johnson quickly jumped out and ran inside. For the past couple of days, his mother and sister had been home, and Johnson had hardly said anything to them—mainly because he was in his room eating chocolate and drinking wine like he always did when he was miserable.

"Mother," Johnson stated as his mom, Nicollet, walked around the wooden living room floor talking on the phone. She raised her hand up, saying one second. Johnson sat down on one of the satin love chairs and waited not one second, but almost ten minutes.

"Yes, Johnson," Nicollet replied. Her raven-black hair was in a neat updo, and she was wearing a silver Prada suit. Before Johnson could even answer, she had her phone in her hands checking her e-mail. Johnson looked around the living room and foyer and noticed many suitcases.

"I don't know if you've read anything about my being depress—"

"They moved my flight up!" Nicollet once again got on her phone. "Flor! Bring me Camber, and get her things ready. We're leaving in five minutes," she shouted. She then turned to Johnson while she waited for her caller to pick up. "I have to go to Paris for that investment meeting. If you need anything, call your grandpa. I'll be back in a week at the most." She grabbed her purse, and her handlers grabbed the rest of the bags. Johnson watched as they packed the limo, and Flor, the nanny, brought down Camber, dressed all in pink ruffles, and went into the limo. Nicollet climbed in without saying 'bye to her son, simply talking to the person she had called. Johnson watched as they drove down the driveway and out the gates.

"Johnson," Theresa, the head maid who lived in the maid suite within the house, said. Johnson turned toward her. "Your medication has arrived." She handed Johnson his long-awaited medication. "Do you want me to get you something?"

"No," Johnson replied as he grasped the bottle with the pills in them. He rushed up to his room and opened the giant doors. Instead of taking the recommended one per day, he took three. As they made their way down his throat and settled, he came to appreciate something. He felt better—way better—with taking more than one pill.

Talan's party that night at his Brickell condo was basically a pool party at the private swimming pool. Every guy was shirtless with board shorts, and every girl had itty-bitty bikinis on. Sasha, Talan, and Jennifer were leaning against the marble wall, drinking chardonnay in fancy glasses. Lorraine, who had had a little too much to drink, was in the swimming pool, a potentially fatal mix. "Is that Johnson?" Jennifer asked, happy to see that he had decided to show up. Well, show up was an understatement. Johnson showed up in a white Calvin Kline T-shirt and board shorts with flip-flops and orange-rimmed sunglasses (despite their being in an indoor swimming pool). Johnson walked over to them, all smiles.

"What's going on?" he asked as he poured himself a glass of chardonnay.

"Johnson?" Sasha asked, still wondering to herself over and over again if he was okay.

"What?" Johnson asked, smiling. He took a sip. Emily ran up to him and embraced her friend.

"I'm so glad you came. Come on, let's swim." She escorted him to the pool.

Meanwhile, back at Lily's place, she and Cliff weren't having as quite as much fun as the rest of the class. After she had finished her cello lesson and practicing the piano, Lily and Cliff sat on her bedroom floor finishing up algebra.

"Okay, we're done with that," Cliff said as he closed his algebra book eagerly.

"You seemed like you were in a rush." Lily smiled as she closed her book.

"Oh, really?" Cliff asked. Lily nodded.

"Now let's see what's on the TV." She got up and got the remote and flicked through the news channels. After a couple of minutes, she settled on the evening news, and Cliff grew some balls.

"We should go to Talan's party," he stated.

"I don't know. Lorraine and Emily are going to be there, and I just don't feel comfortable being there," Lily answered honestly.

"Lorraine won't do anything to you again. I promise," Cliff assured her. Lily smiled.

"Why do you want to go so bad?" she asked.

"I don't," Cliff answered. "I just want to do something fun."

"Well, we did have fun."

"If you can call it that, then yeah, sure, we did have fun," Cliff blandly replied. First couple's fight? Jeez, there have been so many firsts with Lily lately.

"You didn't have fun?" Lily responded, not letting it go.

"I did, but we're young, and we need to have fun. I remember someone telling me that they wanted to experience a lot of things."

"And we will, but I've heard a lot about those parties, and whoever shows up always makes it into *Miami Teen Social*, and if my parents found out I went all the way to Brickell for one of those parties, I would be grounded for life," she admitted.

"We can go and only be there for, like, ten minutes—just enough time to check it out," Cliff suggested.

"I don't think so. Maybe we can pay per view a movie and watch it instead," Lily said, trying to convince him. Cliff sighed. "Or read books?"

"I want to have fun," Cliff finally confessed.

"And what? You don't have fun with me?" Lily almost cried.

"I do, but we're kids. Let's let loose and go to a party," Cliff replied. Lily took a deep breath.

"I don't want to go, and shame on you for trying to force me to go to a party where the girl who attacked me is!"

"God," Cliff moaned as he rolled over.

"I think you should leave," Lily finally stated. Cliff got up.

"I think I will." He got his books and book bag and headed out of Lily's bedroom.

"Have a fun time with Lorraine!" Lily childishly yelled after him.

"I will," he yelled back. Lily screamed and grabbed a pillow and threw it at her door. One word, *"Dang!"*

Back at the party, chardonnay was in full demand as glistening cool bottles came in and empty bottles went out. Emily and Johnson were "entertaining" partygoers at the pool as they danced to whatever music came on. Talan and Sasha made out, and Jennifer danced to the beat of the music. The thing with getting drunk is that people become sloppy and unintentionally may leak out all their secrets, and one little lady is going to have to learn to go to rehab sometime.

"Oh, my God, Jen!" Lorraine shouted as she pranced over to Jennifer, who was dancing while talking to Sasha and Talan.

"What?" Jennifer responded, smiling at her drunken friend.

"Okay, so you're gonna totally laugh when I tell you this, but remember over the summer when Trevor"—that would be Jennifer's ex-boyfriend, the one who moved away, causing Jennifer's heart to shatter—"threw that going-away swimming pool party for himself at the country club?" Jennifer nodded, not sure where the conversation was going. You know, because she was still getting over the move.

"Well, we made out and almost went all the way!" Lorraine blurted out, laughing like some loon maniac. The whole room went quiet as if someone had just relieved himself, letting out a nasty, rank fart. Sasha's jaw dropped in shock at what she had just heard. Talan wanted to burst out laughing at how easy Lorraine was. Emily and Johnson were annoyed that the attention was off them, but soon they grew weary.

"What?" was all Jennifer could say. Her hands were shaking, and she was about to cry.

"Yeah," Lorraine said, giggling. Jennifer let out an eerie scream.

"That was my boyfriend!" she yelled as she got her glass of chardonnay and splashed it into Lorraine's face. Jennifer then grabbed her bag and walked out.

"Did I do something wrong?" Lorraine asked aloud. Everyone just looked at her awkwardly until Hannah came up to her and escorted her to the little ladies' room, hopefully for a good scolding and a cold shower.

The next day at school, even more fights and love were to occur. Yay!

"This weekend went by so fast," Sasha told Emily and Lorraine as they walked into school.

"I know. It was so much fun," Lorraine answered. Lorraine had no shame, and she basically had forgotten what she had confessed to Jennifer. For her part, Jennifer was noticeably absent from the gang, along with the boys, who had decided to stay home to recuperate from the long weekend.

The threesome clacked their way through the main entrance of Hamilton Prep, and a sign met them with a group of students standing around it. Not just any sign, but a sign about one of them.

"Move! What is it?" Lorraine told off a couple of nobodies who were in her way. They moved, and Lorraine's jaw, as well as Emily's and Sasha's, dropped to the hard floor as they read the sign spray-painted on a wall:

LORRAINE LOOSELY EVERLY IS A NASTY WHORE.

"What is this!" Lorraine yelled, embarrassed.

"I'm so sorry, Lorraine. The janitorial staff is painting over it immediately," Headmaster Trimble said, approaching her. Wow. The headmaster even read it. Lorraine didn't care; all she cared about was that people had already seen and read it. She heard some snickering around her. "We're checking security cameras. We'll find who did this," he guaranteed her.

"Take it down now!" she demanded. "My middle name is Leslie, not loosely," she almost whimpered. Lorraine Loosely Everly was the oldest and most brutal joke in the book for a knock out Lorraine day. She looked around and saw Jennifer approaching her. Lorraine's first thought was, *Jennifer did this*, but with one look at Jennifer's distressed face, she knew it couldn't be her.

"I'm sorry," Jennifer stated as she joined Sasha and Emily, who almost looked amused by the whole situation. Lorraine persistently looked around for her culprit, and she soon enough spotted a suspect. In her mind, the guilty suspect was Lily Carrington, who stood by the doors wearing a barrette and toting her Hermes bag.

"Lily, that whore," she snarled. "She'll get it." She turned to her posse.

"What are you gonna do?" Emily asked. Lorraine got out her phone.

"Johnson hates her, and he knows exactly what to do to make her sorry," Lorraine vindictively stated as she seized her phone from her silver handbag.

After a couple classes to cool down the lively events that had taken place that morning, Lorraine put her plan (well, Johnson's plan) into motion. She walked up to Cliff, who was just a couple feet away from Lily, and gave him a big squeeze.

"Oh, I'm so devastated. Did you hear what they did to the wall?" she said dramatically.

"Yeah, I know. Sorry," Cliff answered, somewhat uncomfortable.

"Thanks. Well, just so you know, they're checking surveillance cameras to see who did this!" Lorraine basically bellowed so that Lily would get the message. Lily rolled her eyes and got her books out of her locker. This caused Lorraine to become infuriated and fed up. She ignored Cliff and clacked right after Lily.

"Lily!" she yelled. Lily stopped as she started to walk up the stairs. At the bottom of the stairs, she slowly turned around.

"If you ever write anything about me again, I swear I will kick your ass!" she screamed. A couple of students gathered around, including Cliff, who had caught up to them.

"I didn't write anything about you, and if you would, please, respect me, leave me alone, and stop talking to me." Lily turned back around and made her way up the steps.

"Respect this!" Lorraine yelled as she grabbed Lily's arm and pulled her back.

"Get off of me!" Lily tried to push Lorraine, but Lorraine, being "bigger-boned," had no trouble overcoming Lily, and was already pulling her hair. Aw, such a lady. Lily yelled out in pain, and soon students started to break the two up—again. This time, sadly for Lorraine, teachers were drawn in, and she found herself face-to-face with gray-haired Headmaster Trimble, who had just felt so bad for her earlier.

"It was her," Lorraine pleaded. "She wrote that mean, horrible thing about me," she continued to cry. Blah, blah, blah. What we all want to see is Lorraine Loosely Everly act off against Frizzy Lizzy Van Ryan. Wonder who would win?

"What you did today was inexcusable, Miss Everly," Headmaster Trimble started. "We have the senator calling in to see if his daughter was severely hurt. The senator!" he exclaimed.

"Check the security cams. It was her!" Lorraine still begged. Wouldn't it be wonderful if dear little Miss Lorraine Loosely did end up getting expelled? Oh, how many relationships would blossom without her.

Talan decided to come during lunch, so he wouldn't miss a whole day of school. What a good student! Sasha told him everything that had happened with Lily and Lorraine. All he did was laugh.

"Lily." Lily heard the voice of God—no, not quite God, but close to it. In the eyes of Hamilton faculty anyway, Eleanor Vanderthorn was God.

"Hi, Eleanor," Lily nearly gasped. Eleanor Vanderthorn was Lily's idol; she had wanted to be like her since she could remember. Eleanor was a junior this year, and apart from being the junior class president, she was also student council vice president. Eleanor was the teen dream. "I'm so sorry. I heard about what happened to you earlier today, and I would just like to express my regret." Eleanor gave Lily a big hug. Lily could smell the Chanel perfume streaming off her.

"Thanks, Eleanor." Lily smiled as she got her books out from study hall.

"If you need anything—a shoulder to cry on or an ear to gossip in—here's my cell number," Eleanor said with a smile, handing Lily a piece of paper with her number on it.

"Thanks." Lily couldn't believe her idol had been so kind to her. If it were possible, she had the attitude and brains of Mother Theresa, and the looks and poise of Grace Kelly.

Lily couldn't be any happier. That was, until she walked out into the B quad and walked by Cliff. She tried to smile, and just when she was about to say something, the bell rang. Good old Lily extinguishes every conversation when the bell rings, since she hates being tardy. Cliff simply gave her a friendly wave that made Lily look down in shame as she walked to class; Lily knew she needed to fix things.

"Cliff, sweetie, can you answer that," Susan told her son Cliff as he had just finished changing out of his uniform.

"Yeah, sure," Cliff said as he opened the door. To his amazement, Lily stood at the doorway smiling.

"Hey, Lily," he greeted her awkwardly, but at the same time he was happy to see her.

"I'm sorry how—"

"Lily!" Susan exclaimed. Cliff's mom rushed over to hug her. "Come on in. I'm getting ready for work, but I left Cliff some meat loaf in the oven that I'm sure he won't mind sharing." She laughed. "Oh, and I want to show you my new record player!"

"Okay," Lily answered.

"I bought it for twenty bucks at a flea market earlier," she informed Lily.

"Oh," Lily responded, more eager to talk to Cliff. After Susan finally managed to get off to work, Lily and Cliff sat in the small living room determined to have a serious relationship talk.

"I'm sorry that I got mad at you and told you to leave," Lily started.

"No, it's my fault. Obviously, Lorraine hates you, and today she showed how much. If I would have forced you to go, it would have just been another fight," Cliff apologized. Before another word could be spoken, Lily and Cliff started to kiss. They went into his room for another round of contact. Hopefully, Lily won't be rolling around in pain when she gets home, or else her mother will think it was from the fight she had earlier and they might sue the school for sure.

"Lily!" Lily's mother, Cynthia, rushed up to her daughter once she came home from Cliff's.

"What?" Lily asked, worried that her mom would find out what she had been up to.

"Are you okay?" Cynthia felt her daughter's forehead. "You're all sweaty." Yeah, but from different reasons that weren't on Cynthia's radar.

"Mom"—Lily backed up—"I'm fine. What are you talking about?"

"At school, they said you got into an altercation with some girl, and she pulled your hair." Cynthia touched Lily's hair to make sure it was still as silky as ever.

"Oh," Lily said, "yeah, I'm fine. I'm going to finish reading *The Old Man and the Sea* now. 'Bye." Lily made her way to her room.

As Lily lay on her bed reading Ernest Hemingway, she felt a lot better than she did the last day she experienced the great association with the opposite sex.

"Lily." Lorena, one of Lily's favorite maids, interrupted Lily's reading time. Lily looked up. "A Miss Eleanor Vanderthorn is on the phone for you," she finished.

"Oh," Lily said as she rushed up to answer it, "thank you."

Sasha Chandler was walking along Miami Beach as the sun fell. She loved being out in the sun, and she loved getting her feet wet. She, of course, was on the phone telling Johnson all about what had happened today. One thing that Sasha cherished was the time she spent alone on the beach. Since football season was over, and that was Talan's sport, he didn't want to get out of shape, so he and the guys went to the gym regularly. This year's football season the guys didn't go to state—they almost did, but didn't. So sad. Sports at Hamilton weren't as talked about as the academics, so nobody lost much sleep over it.

"Okay, so he's here. I'll talk to you later," Sasha said to Johnson on the phone as she saw her boy parked in the parking lot along the beach in his convertible 1964 Ferrari 275 GTS. She walked up to the vintage car, and he stepped—well, more like hopped—out and walked over to her.

"Hey, Jace," Sasha addressed him, ready for a long and drama-free night.

"Hey," he gladly replied.

Chapter Thirteen

Love Pentagon

Love triangles are quite attention-grabbing, but if you want to get real complicated, then it's all about love pentagons. Yes, five people in it. It's all an act, just young lust gone bad, and young kids sleeping around, but if everything is kept in the dark, and all STDs and pregnancies are taken care of, then nobody gets hurt all in the name of—fun.

It was Saturday afternoon, and Valentine's Day was right around the corner . . . and right around the corner translates to tomorrow. Talan woke up with none other than his favorite sleepover buddy. He got up and got showered, leaving his partner snoozing in a deep slumber.

"I have to meet Sasha in an hour," he told Emily as she started to wake up from his bed.

"No," she whined, "just stay and let's sleep all day." Then she smiled.

"I wish I could, but I would rather not." Talan changed into a long, loose plaid button-down shirt and black jeans.

"Ugh." Emily rolled around the bed. "When are you going to break up with her already? And you said that you weren't going to date anybody else," she almost sobbed.

"I'm only dating Sasha," he answered as he put on the cologne that made both Sasha and Emily maul him.

"I meant sleeping around," Emily corrected herself.

"What?" Talan replied, almost annoyed. "I haven't slept around with anybody."

"Lorraine!" Emily responded.

"I didn't sleep with her," he answered. Emily rolled her eyes, upset about everything. She was still technically with Faiday, but she didn't like Faiday—he was cute and all, but he wasn't exciting. She was also still pissed when Talan broke off the little fling they had together back at the beginning of the school year when they almost got caught.

"You know the way out," Talan said as he headed out to meet his girlfriend for lunch.

Sasha and Talan met for lunch at Azul, an overpriced cuisine restaurant located inside the Mandarin Oriental Hotel in Brickell. It was a nice place for rich kids to dine, but more significantly, their favorite thing there was a wine list with over seven hundred different kinds of wine. When you have a cash flow like these kids, waiters don't think twice about underage drinking. Not that they noticed, but the restaurant also had an amazing view of the Miami skyline.

"Hey," Sasha greeted him with a warm kiss.

"Hey, babe." Talan sat down. So in all of her annoyingness, Sasha started on a whole spew about what was going on Valentine's Day—all the social events and little dinners, the whole shebang.

"Anyway, I was thinking that you and I should throw our own Valentine's Day party, like, uh, a small sit-down or something," she pitched.

"Uh, sure," Talan replied, busy looking at something on Sasha's body other than her mouth.

"It's going to be awesome. I know it's short notice, but I already have Johnson's event planner on speed dial, and she does a superb job. We won't hand out invites, since duh, it's tomorrow, so we'll just tell them. I was thinking just friends," Sasha went on. The whole time Talan was thinking he could have gotten in another round with Emily if he would have stayed.

Lily and Cliff were swimming in her infinity swimming pool, playing Marco Polo, just the two of them, and they tried to sneak kisses when they could. Lily kept giggling as she thought how funny her mother's face would look like if she were to catch them. It took Cliff forever to understand that he wouldn't fall off the end of the pool. And this is a scholarship kid?

"What do you want to do tonight?" Cliff asked as he drew Lily toward the shallow end of the pool.I don't know. What do you want to do?" she asked, teasing.

"Lily"—Lorena broke in again—"Miss Eleanor is on the phone again."

"Oh." Lily detached herself from Cliff and climbed up the ladder to answer the phone. "Hey, Eleanor," Lily answered as she dried herself with a towel.

Cliff swam around while he waited for Lily to get off the phone.

"That sounds like a plan, and if you need a dress, a whole bunch of Jean Paul Gaultier dresses and gowns just came in from France yesterday. We could try some on to see what looks best . . . yeah . . . okay. I'll see you in an hour." She turned to Cliff as she hung up. "Eleanor just invited me to this homeless youth charity auction, and I'm so excited! I have to wash this chlorine off my skin; thank God I didn't wet my hair. I'll see you tomorrow. Tomorrow you and I will do something," Lily promised as she walked into her house.

"Thanks, Lily, for ditching me, and have fun, too," Cliff jokingly mocked as he climbed out of the pool.

More than a few miles away, at a certain heir's mansion, Sasha Chandler was bragging about Valentine's Day.

"Yeah, and we're going to have dinner at The Palm. We wanted to throw a Valentine's Day dinner party afterward, though—something small, but cute," Sasha notified Johnson, who was on his bed texting.

"Oh, I see," Johnson said, "sounds like fun, fun, fun." Sasha laughed at his amusement.

"Anyway, enough about what I'm doing. What are you going to do?" Sasha asked.

"I don't know. Jen and I, and maybe Lorraine, if I even have to strength to talk to her, are gonna go to Nikki Beach, because they're throwing this cool little party. Then maybe go back to Mansion and see what is going on there."

"Johnson!" Sasha cried. "What about my party?"

"Oh, you haven't invited me, but if you are then I'll go to that."

"You're invited," she said, smiling. "And also I was hoping that you would help me plan it," she eased in, playing with her pale hair.

"What? I thought you and Talan were throwing it."

"It's Talan," Sasha pointed out. Johnson nodded, understanding. "He's not going to want to do anything he doesn't have to do. So please, Johnson, help me out?" Sasha pleaded innocently.

"I guess," Johnson said, giving in to Sasha's charm. So, Johnson and Sasha quickly got on it, calling personal chefs to make one-of-a-kind cuisines and such.

"I think it's just going to be a little get-together for about ten people," Johnson told one of the chefs later on the phone. "So, yeah, I just need like small appetizers, something adorable and flirty-looking, and maybe some jumbo shrimp balls, since everyone likes those," he explained. Meanwhile, Sasha got a text from someone she had been anticipating.

"I have to go. It's Talan," she informed Johnson.

"Okay, hurry back," Johnson said, still on the phone. When Sasha left and Johnson got off the phone, he called his dear friend Jennifer to come and help him out. Once Jennifer came, Johnson spent ten minutes bitching about how he didn't even know the "direction" of the party, so he texted Sasha.

Where are we going to throw it? I don't think I can find a location in one day.

Sasha received the text as she dipped her feet in her sparkling blue swimming pool.

Maybe at your house

"It's nice out, huh?" Jace told Sasha as he lay next to her. Oh, so that text earlier wasn't from Talan after all.

"Yeah, it is," she agreed as she sent her message. Jace gently reached over and stroked Sasha's hand. Sasha's face expressed how she felt, but before she could say anything, Jace had already read her mind.

"You know, we're not cheating or anything," he informed her. Sasha sighed.

"I do know, but I just feel so guilty sneaking around on Talan."

"If you broke up with him and you and I became a couple, then maybe you wouldn't have to sneak around," Jace pointed out. Sasha thought for a moment. She really liked Jace, but she loved Talan. But if she "loved" Talan, then why was she playing with the boundaries with Jace?

"So what are we gonna do for Valentines?" Jace asked. Sasha made a face.

"Talan and I"—go ahead throw that in his face—"are throwing a little party. I'm sorry, but I don't think we can do anything, Jace."

"I really like you," he blushingly admitted. Sasha giggled and looked down into the pool, embarrassed. She liked being around Jace. It was more laid back, yet with a fitting blend of seriousness, unlike being with Talan. "We've been talking now . . . oh, sorry"—he paused—"I mean texting now for a couple weeks, and I hate playing teases and sneaking around. I want it to be more serious," he disclosed. Sasha looked at him.

"Soon, Jace. We will. I'm just so confused right now. Please respect that."

"I do," he acknowledged, "and besides, we're going really slow. The most we've done is me giving you a kiss on the cheek." Sasha laughed. "And that's not where I was intending to kiss you," Jace pointed out, laughing. Sasha and Jace's eyes met for a tender moment, and Jace seized the moment and made another attempt at seduction. The scene was right—a sunny day at a beautiful home, two good-looking kids—but a certain mom was not supposed to be in it.

"Sasha!" Lenny, called out. Sasha quickly jumped up.

"Mom, I thought you were going to have lunch with Irving?" Sasha questioned. Lenny came out of the house looking somewhat civilized in a nice sundress.

"I was, but he canceled. Who's that?" she asked as Jace got up and bobbed on his crutches.

"Oh, it's . . . the new pool boy," Sasha lied as she walked toward Jace and ushered him through the gate.

"What about Ricardo?" Lenny asked.

"Oh, he went on vacation . . . to Cuba . . . and Jace needs money for his alkalis surgery," Sasha continued to lie.

"Well, tell him to be careful when he's around the pool then," Lenny warned. "I don't want anybody getting hurt and suing me for workers' comp."

"Will do." Sasha closed the gate.

Johnson was in a far less good mood than Sasha as he planned the Valentine's party.

"So the people I usually go with are out of town, so I went with these new people. Their foods sound a little iffy, so we're going to have to go do a taste test later on today at five," Johnson informed Jennifer, who was gladly helping him out.

"Sounds great. Where is it going to be?" Jennifer asked.

"I guess here. Sasha texted me and said we should throw it here."

"That's wonderful, because we won't have to decorate anything, since your house is so beautiful." Jennifer ass-kissed.

"I was thinking that we should just have a normal, friendly dinner at the main dining room, and then have white wine, cheese, and chocolate afterward. Then we can go to the party at Mansion," Johnson stated, happy that everything was getting taken care of, even knowing the fact it wasn't his party. "I'm stressed. Let's get some shopping done at Aventura, and then go for lattés," he suggested, smiling.

"Perfect!" Jennifer cheered as she got up from his bed.

"Perfect! That looks so good on you, Lily," another ass-kisser by the name of Eleanor stated.

"Really?" Lily questioned as she composed herself in a dark magenta and satin pink haute couture piece that came in with a collection she and her mother had ordered. "It's not too high-fashion or extravagant, is it?"

"No, absolutely not," Eleanor confirmed as she tried on a simple, playful pink lace dress.

"You girls look marvelous," Cynthia boasted from her chair. Eleanor and Lily were in the fitting room of Lily's mansion trying on dresses for the charity auction they were attending later that evening. In addition to being a professional brown-noser, teen dream, and 4.0 student, Eleanor was also quite the socialite, appearing at multiple social events throughout the year. Cynthia was going to make sure that Lily would follow in the footsteps of Hamilton's most promising upcoming senior.

"Where's Cliff?" Eleanor asked as she got her makeup done by a stylist Cynthia had hired for the night.

"He went home," Lily informed her.

"So, are you guys serious? He's very cute." Eleanor closed her mouth when she saw the look that Lily gave her.

"What?" Cynthia said, laughing. "Cliff and Lily are merely friends. Isn't that right, sweetie?" she asked Lily.

"Of course, Mother," Lily answered. "We're really good friends." Is Lily trying to hide her relationship with Cliff from her parents? He's over enough to make it seem like he's part of the staff, and what about the little articles we write on them? Is Mrs. Carrington ignoring us?

"What about you, Eleanor? How's your relationship with Armistead Brantley?" Cynthia asked.

"Oh, quite fine, actually," she bragged. "Once he graduates from the University of Miami, I will have graduated from Hamilton, and we're both relocating to New York City, where I will attend NYU."

"How wonderful." Cynthia smiled, almost as if Eleanor were her daughter. "Well, I'm having dinner with the mayor and his wife, so I'll see you later, Lily. I hope you girls have a superb evening."

"So," Eleanor asked just after Mrs. Carrington left the room, "what is the deal with you and Cliff?"

"He's my boyfriend, but my mother would kill me if she found out I was dating him," she admitted.

"Oh, well, I guess she won't have to find out then, huh?" Eleanor smiled.

"Yeah," Lily agreed.

"So, do you have any plans for Valentine's Day?" Eleanor asked as the stylist put her dark hair up.

"Yeah, I think Cliff and I might go out somewhere." Lily smiled just thinking about it.

"Aren't you scared your parents will find out? I mean, surely some scumbag tabloid will write about it. 'Senator's daughter out on Valentine's date,'" she mocked. Actually, we would say something more along the lines of, "Good girl Lily Carrington lets loose on Valentine's Day as she and boyfriend, Cliff Bowmen, have a nice, romantic night out on the city".

"No," Lily said, laughing. "When my dad ran for senate, so many false articles were written about him, so if someone on my dad's team tells him there's an article about me on some teen social tabloid, he just shrugs it off," Lily explained.

"Oh," Eleanor responded. "I wish my parents would have shrugged off everything they read about me. Ready?"

At the Annual Homeless Youth Charity Auction, Lily and Eleanor showed up in Lily's chauffeur-driven SUV, and of course the press snapped up pictures of Hamilton's socialite and the senator's daughter. The auction went very well. Lily made a couple bids, and bought a painting, for which she paid $5,000.

"I'm so glad we were able to help raise money for homeless youths," Eleanor told other company. "One thing that really irks me is when kids are homeless and out living in the streets. But I'm glad there are charities such as this one that help them. However, I think it teaches them a life lesson that some of my peers haven't comprehended, and that's that life isn't all about money," she almost campaigned. Lily couldn't believe that a compassionate human being like Eleanor existed.

"That was fun," Lily told Eleanor as they refreshed themselves in the powder room.

"It was," Eleanor agreed. "But," she went on in a more serious tone, "I wanted to talk to you about Cliff. Something is really bothering me," she confessed.

"What is it?" Lily asked, concerned.

"Well, I read the article on Cliff on *Miami Teen Social*, and I just don't think he's appropriate or suitable for you." Lily was both shocked and stunned. She couldn't believe that just hours earlier Eleanor had been bragging about him, saying how adorable he was, and now she had a distaste for him. She also couldn't believe that Eleanor spent time reading *Miami Teen Social*. What is there to say? We pull in a lot of readers.

"I don't understand," Lily responded.

"He doesn't come from money," she answered. Lily's jaw dropped at what came out of Eleanor's mouth. "I know that sounds bad," Eleanor agreed, "but what would you do if your parents found out? You even said yourself that you would be grounded for life if they ever did."

"I love Cliff, and he's my best friend," Lily made Eleanor aware.

"Oh, Lily." Eleanor hugged Lily without Lily hugging her back. "Cliff is probably fun for the moment, but he's no future husband material." Eleanor resumed putting powder on her nose and touching up her makeup. Lily remained frozen.

Talan and Sasha were lying on his bed while he kept up with what was going on with sports center on ESPN. Sasha was on the Internet on her phone looking up some Vivienne Westwood dresses. She snuggled up against the shirtless Talan, whom she "adored."

"I'm going to go get something to eat." Talan got up from the bed and walked out to the kitchen.

"Okay," Sasha said as she too got up, ready to follow him. A sudden pain hit her foot as she stepped onto the cold floor. She looked down to see a bracelet; it wasn't just any old bracelet, though.

"Emily," Sasha said, noticing who it belonged to. The signature silver charm bracelet said it all. She tucked the bracelet in her bag and walked out of the room. "I totally forgot that my mom needs me," Sasha lied, basically holding back tears.

"Okay," Talan said, not even bothering to look, but with his head still in the fridge. Sasha walked out of the condo and into the elevator. While in the elevator, she pulled out her phone and called the one person she wanted to talk to—the one person she needed to talk to. She felt her face become red with irritation and betrayal.

Cliff was in his apartment when he heard a knock at the door. He was watching MTV, and got up to answer it.

"Hey, Lily," he said as he saw his girlfriend, dressed in a fancy dress, standing at the door. Boy, Lily had some balls showing up in a dress in a neighborhood like that.

"Hey," she replied. "Just got back from the charity auction." She stepped inside the apartment, and before Cliff could say anything else, Lily spoke. "I'm happy we're dating, and I wouldn't change you for the world."

"Thanks," Cliff said, smiling. "What made you say that?"

"Just," Lily answered simply. She gradually walked over to Susan's record player and turned it on. An old slow song that Lily wasn't acquainted with came on, and she walked over to Cliff. Lily cleared her throat and straightened up.

"Oh," Cliff said, understanding the situation Lily was producing. "May I have this dance?" he asked politely.

"Of course," Lily answered as she grabbed his hand, and the two charmingly danced around the small living room.

Sasha clung onto Jace with all her strength, crying. They were in his car overlooking the sea on the pier. Jace knew that something was different with Sasha, since she couldn't stop expressing her heartache over something that had happened, but curious as he was, he was determined to not let her remember what had just ensued and was not asking any questions. He just hugged her tight until she finally spoke.

"He's with Emily," she sniffed.

"I'm sorry," Jace said apologetically. Sasha looked up to Jace, and their eyes met. Almost immediately, she pressed her lips against his. Jace took a deep breath and continued to kiss her, but soon stopped.

"No," Jace said, backing up. Sasha glanced at him. "Not like this, Sasha." Sasha nodded, knowing how the situation looked . . . Jace looked like the rebound.

"I'm sorry." Sasha leaned against his chest and closed her eyes. Soon she heard nothing, saw nothing. Jace, unfaltering, was falling asleep in his car, with Sasha sound asleep on him.

"Goodnight." He kissed her on the cheek and closed his eyes.

Sasha awoke the next day to sounds of seagulls, cars honking on the nearby highway, the ocean pounding against the beams below them, but more importantly, to the sweet sound of Jace's soft snoring. She got up from him, but as she did he came around and slowly stretched.

"Sorry," she apologized.

"It's okay," he assured her, smiling.

"Happy Valentine's Day." She kissed Jace softly on his lips, but this time Jace kissed back.

"I should get you back home," Jace said, stroking Sasha's chin.

As Sasha walked into her house, she abruptly felt sad. Not only was she not with Jace, but the house—her home—brought back painful memories. She hated being there. The house made her feel guilty. She also committed to the memory that all along she was a fool. Talan was sleeping with one of her best friends. Sasha had been the good girl all her life, never making fun of people, always obeying her mother's rules (which were not many), and pleasing her loved ones. This time she was going to strike a strong pose. Sasha walked up to her bathroom and took a shower. She glumly curled her long platinum-blond hair, and dolefully did her makeup. She zipped up in a bright yellow dress by Oscar de la Renta, and threw on some pink Bebe booties. She waited until it was seven, sitting on her satin vanity holding Emily's bracelet—the epitome of a broken heart. Her driver took her to The Palm, which was an interesting choice for a romantic dinner; it was romantic, but also very laid-back. Seems like Jace's laid-back approach to life had rubbed off on the ritzy model's daughter.

"Babe, you look great." Talan kissed Sasha tenderly on the lips. Sasha intentionally made her lips tense; the horror that the smell of Emily would be on his breath made her sick. Talan was dressed up in the standard black button-down shirt and black slacks, but this time he wore a dark gray blazer. The accessory on his wrist was a Cartier watch. Talan looked around the place, which had cartoons drawn on the walls.

"Why did you choose this place?" he asked.

"Because I like it, and it has silly vibe, but yet romantic," she answered.

"Oh, here. I forgot." Talan handed Sasha a dozen red roses wrapped beautifully.

"Thanks." Sasha set them aside. Once they ordered, Talan and Sasha (well, mostly Talan) talked. Sasha just nodded and smiled every once in a while. She loved Talan, she really did, but he had just betrayed her, and the only thing she thought about was how she wanted to see Jace. Every once in a while, she would excuse herself and go to the restroom. Possibly calling Jace?

"Okay, so are we just gonna go to Johnson's?" Talan asked as he took a bite from Sasha's cheesecake. It's a well-known fact that the cheesecakes at The Palm are flown all the way from New York . . . just a little cool fact.

"No, I have to go back to my house and change," she replied.

"What? You look perfectly hot." Talan smirked.

"Thanks, but I had another outfit planned. See you there," Sasha said as she got up.

"I'll just go with you," Talan responded.

"No, it's okay."

"No, I will." Talan came up and put his arms around Sasha's waist. "Besides, I want us to have some alone time."

"Okay." Sasha blinked. Was she going to meet up with Jace? Naughty.

Back at Sasha's house, her mom of course was out on a date with a guy, or even perhaps *guys*. Talan grabbed Sasha's arm and kissed Sasha overpoweringly once they were in the comfort of her bedroom.

"Talan," Sasha groaned, "I have to get dressed."

"So," Talan said as he took off his blazer and fell on top of Sasha on her bed.

"Talan," Sasha said, trying to push him off, "I have to get ready."

"No, you don't," he answered, almost irritated that someone didn't want to sleep with him.

"Talan!" Sasha finally snapped.

"What the hell is your problem? What's wrong with you?" Talan asked, pissed. Sasha removed herself from under Talan and walked to her walk-in closet.

"I'm not in the mood, and I told you!" she explained harshly. Tissues, anyone? So proud that Sasha is standing up for herself.

"You have serious problems, Sasha," Talan bitterly said as he got his blazer.

"No, you do. Because you don't know when no is no," Sasha clarified, getting a BCGC dress out of her closet.

"If you're going to act like this, then you can act like this by yourself. When we go to that stupid party, you'd better straighten up, and tonight you're staying the night at my house," Talan said, glaring.

"Sorry, but my mom wants me to stay home for once." Sasha teased Talan by taking off her dress right in front of him.

"Yeah, right, like your mom even knows where you are. I'm waiting out in the God damn car. Hurry up." He walked out of the room frustrated. Sasha took a deep long-awaited breath as he left. Sasha knew that she wasn't going to be played around by anyone, and if Emily thought she was going to be her friend, she was sorely mistaken! Sasha put on her BCGC ruffled silk dress and exchanged her booties for stilettos.

The ride to Johnson's house was more than hushed and awkward. Talan texted Emily on his phone, and Sasha texted Jace on her phone. Once they got there, it was time to act as if they were happy and perfect, when they were feeling far from that.

The night was an extravagant, fun one. Jennifer, Lorraine—and who could forget about Emily—came in wearing pretty flirty cocktail dresses, with lovely heels. Faiday and Johnson looked refined and sophisticated, with a pinch of sexy in Calvin Klein wear. Regardless of everyone drinking wine, nibbling on expensive entrées, and marveling over Johnson's house, Sasha's eyes were chock-full of repulsion, love, and not-so-happiness. She looked at Emily with disgust. She hated her. She absolutely hated her. During dinner, she almost gagged when Emily talked about her friends. Sasha turned to look at Johnson, and her eyes filled with love. She loved her friend. She was gratified to see that he was one of the only people who were ever truly there for her. Sasha felt like her life was going nowhere. She looked like a future supermodel, and had the bank account of an heiress, but it wasn't enough for her to be happy. She turned to Talan next to her, her eyes turned to not-so-happy. How could someone she absolutely adored betray her like that? Sleeping with her friend was low, a really low hit!

Sasha finished up her last glass of wine before facing Talan.

"I have to go home now," she established, still trying to smile and make it seem like it was just normal "I love you" chitchat.

"What?" he almost growled. He's really making this easy for Sasha; he's just basically showing her the way to Jace.

"Knock it off," she countered at the sound of his voice.

"Everyone is going to Nikki Beach, and I'm not going without you."

"Well, don't go, do go. I don't really care. I have to get home." She turned around. "I'm sorry, guys, but my mom has this crazy emergency, so I have to get home," she informed them indly.

"Is everything okay?" Jennifer asked.

"Yeah," Sasha smiled; then she turned to face Talan. "It will be."

"Jace!" Sasha rushed up to him as he waited by her front door. "I missed you." She kissed him on his lips, and the two kissed for what seemed like hours. They met up at Sasha's house, which they had all to themselves.

"I missed you too," he agreed, hugging her. Sasha kicked off her heels once they got in the refuge of her house, and they both lay down on Sasha's bed, talking. Sasha just smiled, taking in the moment of listening to Jace tell her about his day. She and Talan always talked about what he did, and his day. Next, Jace said something that she wasn't used to Talan saying.

"Who cares about what I did? What about your day?" he asked. Sasha took in a deep breath before telling him.

"I really like you, Jace," Sasha concluded. Jace smiled. "But I can't break up with Talan," she stated. Jace sighed heavily and frowned. "Not just yet. I have to do something. Trust me." Sasha sealed her sentence with a kiss.

Was that love pentagon thirst-quenching enough? How long it will last is anybody's guess, if more people join in . . . well, that's certainly for sure. And will the people in it get hurt? Well, when the love pentagon becomes public, chaos will erupt. Love pentagons are like playing with fire. Someone is always bound to get burned. This is *Miami Teen Social*, signing off.

Chapter Fourteen

Cliques

Cliques—they are essential to the life of any rich kid. They define who one is. For the kids of Hamilton Prep, cliques are everything. They are fun, competition, love, and jealously all together in a tight closeness. Just like in any other cliques, there are ranks and those who get left out, especially if one plans strategically.

"So, I'm going to Dadeland for some shopping, and then I'm getting new extensions because these are heinous. Then I'm off to the spa, and you guys should totally join me. We could all go eat somewhere afterward, too," Sasha deliberately told Johnson, Jennifer, and Lorraine as Emily walked over. What's more obvious—Sasha plotting something against Emily Parker, who she recently found out was sleeping with her boyfriend Talan Merrick, or Sasha saying she's going to eat somewhere? When does Sasha eat?

"Dadeland?" Emily spoke as she sat down. "Ooh, I wanna go." Sasha gasped.

"Oh, my God. Sorry, Emily," Sasha started, sounding "wretched." "I was such an idiot, and only booked four reservations for the spa. They said there was barely enough room, because I was also going to invite Hannah," she lied.

"Oh," Emily said, disappointed, "it's okay."

"Well, I'm sure there's someone you can do," Sasha retaliated. Emily laughed.

"You mean something?" she asked as she drank her diet soda.

"Nope," Sasha responded, smiling.

"Look, Lily," Bernice Anderson, one of Lily and Cliff's more nerdy friends, declared as she looked at her phone.

"What?" Lily responded as she sat up from lying on Cliff.

"There's an article about you on *Miami Teen Social*." She smiled with her braces popping out of her mouth.

"Ugh," Lily moaned.

"I want to know what it says," Cliff pointed out.

"Okay, read it," Lily told Bernice. And so, Bernice read the article.

> Whenever one thinks of homeless youth charities, they think of people who want to help out. For poor Lily Carrington, daughter of the senator, helping out is showing up to a homeless youth charity auction over Valentine's weekend wearing a $12,000 Jean Paul Gaultier haute couture dress. What the heck was she thinking!! It was a charity auction, not a fashion viewing. These poor kids haven't even seen $12 shirts, let alone a $12,000 dress. But to help, she did buy a $5,000 painting. Now with that she could have bought approximately 416 shirts! Let's hope she doesn't show up to another *charity* auction wearing pricey couture pieces.

> Comments—

> Fruitloops says—OMG, she's totally crazy. That's so mean and retarded. That's like someone giving condoms to AIDS victims. It's rubbing it in their faces that they're below her, and she has money. She is starting to become so snobby.

<u>Adam/Eve</u> says—I thought she looked amazing in that dress, and nobody should hate on her cuz she is da only decent one in that whole freakin' school.

Lily was utterly shocked as Bernice read the article along with the comments.

"What? That is so mean," Lily stated, looking upset.

"Don't listen to them. You gave them $5,000," Cliff said soothingly.

"Eleanor said it was a perfect outfit, and she's been to tons of events," Lily said doutbfully.

"Well, they're just jealous." Cliff smiled as he kissed Lily on her cheek. "Are we going to hang out tonight?" he asked.

"Of course." Lily smiled and rested her head on his shoulder, still annoyed over the article.

"Mother," Lily complained as she handed her mom the phone with the article on it as soon as she got home. Cynthia read it and wheezed.

"Don't pay any attention to that. All they do is point out the flaws," she affirmed. "They did the same thing to your father."

"Hold on," Lily said as she read a text from her phone. "It's Eleanor," she stated after a while. "She wants me to go to a gallery opening downtown."

"Oh, that would be just a perfect time to redeem yourself, honey. I got this dress, and I think you would look so causal, yet classy."

"Okay," Lily breathed. "Let me call Eleanor so she can come over and help us," Lily said, forgetting all about her plans with Cliff and heading off to the fitting room.

While Lily got dressed, a clique was having some dinner after a hard day at the spa and salon. It seemed that some suspicious actions were going on. After visiting the spa and getting her hair done, Sasha abruptly left the clique and said she had an emergency. Tired of waiting, Johnson called Emily so she wouldn't feel left out, given that, after all, they were done with the spa and were now heading off to eat. They were eating at the fabulous French restaurant Palme D'Or, at the historic Baltimore Hotel, gossiping and whatnot, when Sasha reappeared. After paying almost $2,000 for a couple new extensions, styling, and a new dye job (which was her usual platinum-blond color), her hair was in a messy bun, and she looked worn out and almost sticky with sweat. Ewww.

"Sorry, guys. Talan needed me for something," she stated as she sat down. Emily's face twisted with confusion.

"You left us for Talan?" Johnson questioned, annoyed. By her appearance it was obvious she had had an afternoon quickie.

"Sorry, it was an emergency." Sasha turned to a waiter walking by and ordered her usual salad and water.

"Hey, Sasha," Emily greeted her. Sasha "warmly" smiled back while texting. Johnson, Jennifer, and Lorraine felt an awkward shudder go through the group. Boy, haven't things turned around for the group. At the beginning it was Emily who couldn't care less about her friendship with Sasha, publicly admitting she was with Talan, and now she was . . . craving her seal of friendship.

Talan was lifting weights (This time for real. He wasn't fibbing and trying to be sneaky with the girls.) with a couple of his friends at the gym at his condo in Brickell Key. Faiday, one of his best friends/Emily's boyfriend, Ashton Cross, and the rest of the guys were talking about none other than their girlfriends, and as such gentlemen do, how often they put out. Something their mothers would be so proud of.

"Sasha, at least three times a week," Talan bragged as he bench-pressed. All the guys laughed their douchy laughs.

"Damn, Emily not very often. Well, not as much anyway," Faiday stated as he took a break and took a swig out of his water bottle, sounding depressed. Talan silently laughed, knowing why she didn't. The thing with guys and cliques was that there really wasn't a personal emotional level. With girls one word could upset the whole crowd, and cause each one to turn around and backstab the other, but with guys the real amusement was not so much scheming but, in its place . . . actual physical combat. Even rich boys know how to brawl.

"Lorraine?" Sasha whispered as they all shopped at Dadeland.

"Yeah," she replied, not getting the quiet part. Sasha rolled her eyes.

"Let's take a walk." Sasha clutched Lorraine's arm, and they walked farther down the shopping scene. "So, I've been thinking, and I know how things are kind of falling apart between you and Richard." Richard was a sophomore whom Lorraine was gravely trying to chase (literally), but subsequent to Lorraine's little scuffle with the senator's daughter, his parents advised him not to see her anymore, and so he didn't.

"Yeah," Lorraine repeated, fascinated by what she had to say.

"And I think you should date . . . Faiday," Sasha happily stated.

"What?" Lorraine responded, alarmed. "No, no, I can't."

"And why not?" Sasha said, irritated.

"He's dating Emily," she explained. Wow, like that stopped her from making out with Talan.

"Listen," Sasha started, "there are people that you know are meant to be together, and people that aren't. Emily and Faiday aren't meant to be together, and I see the way he looks at you," she teased.

"Really?" Lorraine said, eating all of Sasha's BS.

"Yes," she said, smiling. "Just promise me you'll talk to him," Sasha pleaded.

"I dunno, Sasha. I don't think he's into me."

"You know how they are, Lorraine! They're going to break up one minute and then try to get back together the next. But if Faiday has someone . . . more experienced in physical naughty interactions, then he won't let there be another minute for Emily," Sasha fed her. Lorraine smiled, marveling at the fact that she could be with Faiday Hayward, the bad boy of their clique. She always had a thing for the bad boys.

"Hey, there you girls are," Emily said as she saw them.

"Don't say anything. It might upset Emily," Sasha reminded Lorraine.

"Right," Lorraine agreed, nodding.

While Lily was at a gallery opening showing off another piece of the Jean Paul Gaultier collection, Cliff was miserable at home playing video games with his friends, all the while receiving texts from Lily saying how sorry she was that they couldn't hang out. Cliff replied with coy answers. At the moment, Sasha and Talan were doing something that Cliff probably wished he and Lily could do more of.

"You were amazing." Talan smirked as he closed his eyes.

"Thanks," Sasha replied timidly. "I really love you, Talan," she soon professed like she was on her deathbed. Talan almost felt taken aback at her serious tone. Sasha had really turned up the heat for Talan. She had almost gone out of her way to make him happy.

"I know we're young, but I want to be together forever," Sasha said intently, playing with the ring he had given her. Her phone suddenly rang.

"Oh, it's Johnson. He's on suicide watch again." She quickly got up from Talan's bed and went to his bathroom.

"Hey, babe," she whispered. Really? Johnson?

"I'm with . . . Johnson, and he's throwing one of his tantrums, so I can't talk. I'll call you right when I leave," she basically lied to Jace as she hung up and went back to Talan. She went back and lay down next to him, and turned back to her captivating lure.

"I'm sorry about that," Sasha mumbled.

"No, it's okay. Is he going to be all right?" Talan asked.

"Yeah, he is, but I really want us to work through our problems, Talan." Sasha continued to speak softly. "And I just want us to be 100 percent all right, because I love you that much. I want to make you absolutely happy. I hate when we fight. It makes me feel like . . . well, like how Johnson probably feels right now." Talan struggled to swallow as a lump appeared in his throat.

"I'm sorry if I've done anything to hurt you," he almost grumbled as he hugged Sasha tighter.

"It's okay. I love you, Talan, and forgive everything you've done. I'll always forgive you."

"I love you, too," he finally responded. After almost seven months of dating, he at last said the L word. She once more lay her head against his chest and smiled, relishing the fact that he had said he loved her, and it was in the end all going to blow up in his face.

Sasha left Talan's. Talan, for all intents and purposes, didn't want her to leave. He said he wanted her to "stay forever, and never leave." How adorable and sweet. Anyway, Sasha had her driver take her to none other than Lorraine's house, despite it being past midnight. A schemer's work is never done. Lorraine's Japanese maid escorted Sasha to Lorraine's bedroom, where she was on the floor looking through some old CDs.

"Sasha," she stated, happy to see her. She got up off the floor.

"Lorraine," Sasha said and hugged her.

"What's up?"

"I wanted to talk to you more about Faiday." She smiled. "We should invite him over," she suggested as she held up her phone. Lorraine beamed, knowing that possibly she and Faiday could have a consistent relationship, unlike his and Emily's. Sasha must be truly convincing, because since when do any of Lorraine's relationships last?

Guilt is a tricky thing. It can eat and eat at someone's insides until they have nothing to do, except to resolve the dilemma and let everything out. Even Hamilton Prep kids have guilt and a conscience.

"What are you saying?" Emily questioned as she and Talan talked in an empty classroom the following day.

"I'm saying it's over—again," Talan responded, feeling really chaotic and stressed out.

"You're not going to break up with me again, Talan," Emily said, on the verge of tears.

"I can't do this anymore," Talan ended as he walked out of the classroom. Emily sat in one of the desks crying. She wanted Talan more than anything, and she felt like he was going to break up with Sasha any day.

What Lily wanted more than anything, was for *Miami Teen Social* to stop picking on her wardrobe.

"I can't believe this! Not again," Lily pouted as she showed Cliff and her gang yet another article on our website about her.

> Will Lily Carrington ever hire a stylist? That is today's question and poll. The senator's daughter showed up to an event last night dressed like a Korean foreign exchange student who has never heard of American fashion. Lily showed up in yet another creation by her favorite French designer, Jean Paul Gaultier. This time, she appeared in a pink baby doll dress that seemed to be out of the closet of Courtney Love. She looked absolutely ridiculous. She went with fellow Hamilton Prep student, and Miami teen socialite, Eleanor Vanderthorn, who looked gorgeous in a one-shouldered dress by the same designer. Gosh, at the rate she is going, Lily is going to crack the top five worst-dressed socialites in Miami this year.
>
> Comments~
>
> DJ-Deb says—LMFAO, and not the band! She looked utterly hilarious in that baby doll dress. I can't believe she wore that. And so true that does look like something Courtney Love would wear.
>
> K!KI says—I didn't think she looked all that bad in it. She looked cute and adorable. But I do think it was way

inappropriate for a gallery opening. I'm surprised they let her in, but she is the senator's daughter.

KalaD says—Why does she hang out with Eleanor but dress nothing like her? She needs to calm down with the expensive nasty dresses and just go for something plain.

"They hate me," Lily muttered. "I am going to make the worst-dressed list for sure. Everyone is going to make fun of me."

"No," Cliff said, holding her. He soon started to laugh.

"What's so funny?" Lily complained.

"I just really liked that dress you wore," he said, smirking.

"Really?" she asked.

"No, not really." He finally burst out laughing. "Why would you wear that?" he asked shortly, holding back his out-of-control laughter and looking at the picture.

"Eleanor said I would turn heads and give off a youthful vibe," Lily explained.

"Well, we're going to give off youthful vibes tonight, since we haven't hung out in so long," Cliff said while cradling Lily.

"I know," Lily moped.

After school, while one of her guys was off at the gym and the other at a rehab center working out his ankle, Sasha needed a break from all her devious lies, and was with her friends. Emily was noticeably absent . . . again. They were in Johnson's bedroom playing with his chinchilla, Chutney, who was like five years old and needed to be put down. Sasha was pleased that Lorraine was texting Faiday. In this generation, texting a guy is equivalent to "seriously talking." Sasha, nonetheless, was even more pleased that Talan was texting her every minute that they were apart, saying how much he loved and missed her.

"Why doesn't she move that much?" Lorraine grumbled as she threw a toy so Chutney could go after it. It's not a dog, Ms. Lorraine.

"Her leg was broken just a couple months ago, and she's a wee bit elderly," Johnson explained in plain words. As Johnson, Sasha, Jennifer, and Lorraine all had laughs, giggles, and tittle-tattles, Emily was far from that as soon as she arrived, unannounced.

"What's wrong, Emily?" Johnson asked, alarmed.

"Faiday broke up with me," she cried. Ouch, getting dumped by two guys in one day.

"What? Why?" Johnson asked as he and Jennifer went to comfort her.

"He said that he wanted to 'explore his options,'" she whimpered, with full quotation gestures. She sat down on the edge of Johnson's bed.

"I'm sorry," Jennifer said sympathetically while rubbing her friend's hand.

"Tonight, we're all gonna go out, and you'll find an even hotter guy," Johnson said, trying to cheer her up.

"I don't want another guy!" Emily cried as she buried her face into a pillow. Sasha and Lorraine looked at each other mischievously and soon joined the others on the bed who were trying to please Emily.

What is within a clique? Love, hatred? If cliques are meant to be a close link between friends, then why all the scheming and hurt? Then again, cliques aren't supposed to last forever. This is *Miami Teen Social*, signing off.

Chapter Fifteen

Sabotage

Sabotage is a very essential layer to obliteration. Sabotage normally is understandable; someone hates someone, and then sets them up, and *boom!* Sabotage happens. But in the elite society of Hamilton Prep, sabotage is kept secret and revealed only to those who are a part of it. Because in the end, when someone gets obliterated, it always hurts more when she doesn't see it coming.

"Would you please go with me to my boyfriend's friends' band concert?" Eleanor invited Lily as they walked to their own private vehicles after school.

"Tonight?" Lily asked.

"Yes, please," Eleanor continued, "and it would be a great chance for you and Armistead to meet."

"Sorry, but Cliff and I were going to hang out," Lily tried to explain.

"Lily," Eleanor stated firmly, "you said that you wanted to learn the ropes of becoming a socialite, and going to a chill concert is going to make you appear less stuck-up."

"Okay," Lily responded, not recalling when she told Eleanor all that. "But I promised Cliff," she added sincerely.

"Please," Eleanor almost pleaded. Keep in mind Ms. Eleanor is a socialite and pleading is beneath her. "I don't want to be the only girl."

"Okay, fine. I'll go," Lily agreed, finally breaking down.

After an extended afternoon of shopping, Sasha returned to her home. Of course, the only reason she came was because a new couple was taking a dip in her pool, hiding their new relationship.

"Lorraine," Sasha called as Lorraine and Faiday kissed on the edge of the pool, but not before taking a couple minutes to marvel at Faiday in his trunks. If only she could cut out Lorraine, it would be perfect. Lorraine quickly got up and walked to her leader. Slow down, Lorraine. We sure wouldn't want you to fall and hurt yourself (at least not today, anyway).

"Yes," Lorraine replied, happy that she and Faiday were hitting it off, "and before you say anything else, you were totally right on having us meet in private and getting to know each other before anything serious went on. We've already done it tw—"

"Yeah," Sasha interrupted, not wanting to know the gory details. "Your mom would be so proud," she mumbled as she looked at Faiday, who was still on the edge of the pool smiling at her.

"What?" Lorraine asked as she looked back from staring at Faiday. Sasha quickly averted her gaze.

"You should be so happy that it worked out. I am. I was thinking that you guys should take your relationship to the next level."

"Meaning?"

"Meaning you guys should go out in public to make it official," Sasha clarified.

"But Emily might find out."

"And so what? They're done. Well, bah, I have to go meet Talan," she ended as she kissed Lorraine, waved at Faiday, and headed out.

"I'm wearing what you suggested," Lily told Eleanor on the phone as Davie made his way to pick her up. The very smart Lily had foolishly accepted styling tips from Eleanor once again. This fashion column is going to be so much fun, scrutinizing her wardrobe—again.

"Good," Eleanor replied on the other end of the phone. "You don't want people to think you're uptight."

"I know," Lily agreed just as Davie opened her door for her.

When Lily finally made it to the concert and met up with Eleanor, her jaw plunged to the dirty ground. She and Eleanor in absolutely no way looked alike, as Eleanor had promised they would. Eleanor was dressed in black Prada slacks, an off-white top, and a blazer. Her hair was neatly pulled back, and she had drooping earrings. Lily, on the other hand—on the guidance of Eleanor—showed up in very short, faded Daisy Duke shorts (almost to the point of denim underwear) and a midriff-revealing tank top, and she had on a pair of boots to top the look. In good old Lily style, she had on Chanel earrings that didn't sit well with the rest of her whole whore outfit.

"Eleanor," Lily stated, self-conscious about the way she looked, "I look bad."

"No, you don't," Eleanor comforted her. "You look terrific. Armistead," she called. Just then a strapping, light brown-haired Armistead Brantley appeared, looking causal in a polo shirt and some jeans. "Armistead, this is Senator Carrington's only child, Lily," she said, introducing them. Lily was almost insulted that Eleanor used the word *child* in introducing her.

"It's very nice to meet you." Armistead extended his long arm, and Lily shook it, still feeling uneasy about her outfit. She felt even more uneasy when she noticed Armistead looked her up and down, and grinned. Lily took back her hand.

"It's very pleasant to make your acquaintance." Lily tried to smile.

"Okay, so we have tickets for the front row, and then we can all chill later," Armistead suggested. Lily almost dismissed the way he looked at her earlier when she found out how different and less snobby he was than Eleanor . . . more cool and human. She also dismissed her concern about Eleanor's advice on how to dress, because Eleanor was right—this outfit was making her less uptight.

"Sounds great to me," Lily agreed.

"No, no, no." Eleanor shook her head, not amused with the whole pitch. "I have to get up early tomorrow because my parents and I are going to a luncheon, and I have to look my absolute best. And don't forget we're having dinner tomorrow night," Eleanor reminded Armistead, who appeared to be uninterested in the social scene. Lily almost giggled when she saw that Armistead rolled his eyes.

"Something funny?" Eleanor asked, not understanding.

"Let's go take our seats, ladies," Armistead interjected. When Eleanor started to walk and Lily followed, Lily felt an arm feel at her backside; she looked up to see Armistead. Once again she felt discomfort. Throughout the whole show, Armistead's hand would only "accidentally'" stroke Lily's hand almost half a dozen times. Lily felt her stomach do flip-flops as she looked at Eleanor, who seemed almost oblivious to anything going on. Only Lily was wrong—Eleanor saw everything that was going on.

"Is Lily going with us?" Armistead asked Eleanor as she got ready for their date the next night.

"No, why would she be going with us?" Eleanor snapped as she put on her mascara.

"I don't know." Armistead threw his hands up in defense. "You guys are always together, so I thought she would be joining us." Eleanor sighed heavily as she looked at herself in her mirror.

"You know, I'm not feeling well. We should reschedule," she said.

"Okay, are you sure?" Armistead asked, rolling his eyes. He hated dressing up. It was Eleanor's precise direction. She always wanted to seem so perfect, and he hated it.

"Yeah, I have an even better idea," she mumbled so that Armistead couldn't even hear a word.

"Fine." Armistead gently kissed Eleanor on her cheek before exiting her room. Eleanor waited until he left, and then she walked over to her phone and dialed Cliff Bowmen's number.

Eleanor wasn't the only one scheming that night. Sasha was letting her imagination run wild on how Emily's face would look when she read about her ex-boyfriend hooking up with one of her best friends shortly after their breakup. Sasha, Talan, Lorraine, and of course Faiday were at LIV drinking wine, dancing, and enjoying being young—very young.

Sasha made sure that Faiday and Lorraine had drinks in their hands at all times. She knew that Lorraine was a sloppy drunk and wanted her to mount Faiday for all the photographers to see. Sasha, too, had to have her fun, so while she had Talan wrapped around her finger (funny how things work out) she was texting Jace.

"I love you," Talan confirmed once again as he danced with Sasha at an extremely close distance, almost as if they were in a blizzard freezing to death.

"I know," Sasha teased, remembering that once upon a time he would say that to her.

"Hey, Eleanor," Cliff greeted her as he saw Eleanor on one of the piers at Miami Beach. It was almost eleven thirty, and on a school night. *What are these overachievers thinking?* Eleanor had dressed down from the outfit she was wearing earlier and was dressed in track suit—a $300 one, but it's still an improvement.

"Hey." She gave Cliff a warm hug, and waited a couple seconds before letting go.

"So, where's Lily?" he asked. Eleanor had called Cliff and told him that he should join Lily and her for a walk on the beach, and he gladly accepted.

"I've been calling her for the last fifteen minutes, but she won't answer," she lied. "Such a shame; it's a beautiful night for a walk. Don't you think?" she asked.

"Yeah, it is. Let me try calling her," he asked.

"No," Eleanor stated rather quickly. "I left messages and stuff, so she's probably on her way, or she might be a little tied up. Let's just go on without her."

"Okay," Cliff responded, not sure what to think.

"Come on." Eleanor grabbed Cliff's hand, and they both walked toward the beach. *Oh, gosh, the socialite holding hands with the poor peasant boy. Eleanor is improving.*

The next day at school, the argument that everyone spent the whole day talking about happened at nine o'clock. Lily saw Emily clacking her way toward Lorraine, Sasha, Johnson, and Jennifer, in very chic, gold Manolo Blahniks, which Lily had to have. Johnson then heard Emily yell at Lorraine like he was accustomed to on Friday nights, when his booth was taken. After that, Jennifer heard Lorraine yell back some words in her defense, some words that her mother would not be fond of. At that time, Sasha saw Emily smack Lorraine, and as Lorraine cringed, so did Sasha.

"Stop!" Sasha disciplined them as she held Lorraine back, trying to prevent her from hitting Emily as she walked away. "You already got suspended once for fighting," she reminded her as Lorraine sniveled in frustration.

As Cliff was in awe at seeing two beautiful girls go at it, he turned to his girl, who he thought was just as beautiful, and asked her a question.

"What was up with last night?" he asked.

"What are you talking about?" Lily asked, still smiling that Lorraine had just been slapped right across her face. It served her right.

"Last night, when you ditched us," he informed her.

"What?" Lily asked, baffled over what her boyfriend was talking about.

"Last night you didn't show up to . . ." Cliff faltered as he saw Eleanor approaching them.

"I have the best idea for you, Lily," Eleanor interrupted as she basically came in between Lily and Cliff.

"What?" Lily said, annoyed, as she still wanted to find out what on earth Cliff was talking about.

"They are now taking in submissions for student council elections, and since you are going to be a sophomore next year, you can run for something. I was thinking secretary," Eleanor enlightened Lily as she took her away and they walked down the hall. Cliff sighed and got his books and followed behind them like a puppy.

At lunch, things took an interesting turn. Everyone was talking about the not-speaking clique seated opposite one another in the lunchroom.

On one side you had Johnson, and beside him Emily and Jennifer. Then on the other side you had Sasha, Talan, Lorraine, and Faiday.

"This is totally retarded," Johnson stated, overwhelmed by the whole situation.

"I know," Jennifer agreed.

"I can't believe Lorraine is with Faiday," Emily sobbed, unresponsive to anything else.

"Lorraine only cares about herself," Johnson told her soothingly. "She dates anybody and anything. You're prettier and skinnier," he said, smiling.

"Like that helps much," Emily angrily acknowledged as she got up and walked out of the cafeteria.

"You did your best, Johnson," Jennifer chipped in. Johnson nodded before getting back to texting Sasha.

"We should go sit with them," Sasha informed her table.

"No!" Lorraine basically screamed. Sasha drew back, but then quickly regained her poise.

"Don't yell, Lorraine," she stated firmly. "If you want to act like you're two, then you can sit by yourself."

"Sorry, Sasha, but they probably talked so much crap about me, and if I see Emily one more time, I swear to God I'm going to hit her," Lorraine swore like the lady she was. Talan and Faiday both just stared out into the sky, bored, ignoring what was going on. All they knew was that they had girlfriends and were getting some.

Instead of paying attention to the divided clique everyone was spending so much time talking about, Lily and Eleanor were on the topic of strategy for student council elections. Lily had signed up to run for secretary, and there was no backing out now. Eleanor, of course, was a shoo-in for president.

"I think we should get some buttons, and make a lot of posters that say, 'A good school is a good student council committee. And a good student council candidate is Lily Carrington!'" Eleanor pitched. Judas priest, is she serious? She looked at Lily to see her feedback, and scared of throwing her off her mighty horse, Lily quickly smiled and nodded. Cliff was just as uninterested as Talan and Faiday but just overlooked it, realizing he was getting some, too.

That day after school, Sasha just felt so appalled about the day's events that she went over to Johnson's to talk about it—you know, since Sasha has such high moral standards and not any bit of this was her fault. More importantly, however, Sasha was hurting inside, and all of the scheming and plotting was tearing at her heart.

"I feel so bad about what's going on," she told Johnson. "Just because Emily and Lorraine are fighting doesn't mean we should have to pay the price and not be able to talk to each other," she let out.

"I know," Johnson established, appearing lost in thought about something else. Sasha took a deep breath, as she was about to tell her friend everything that was going on, but she stopped once his phone rang.

"Dr. Kimp," Johnson answered like he had been waiting years for her to call. "Excuse me," he said to Sasha as he left the room. Sasha started milling around her friend's room, which she was familiar with. She was searching for lotion, but what she found were four empty medicine bottles.

"Prozac," Sasha read. *Jeez, how much does he need?* she asked herself as she shortly found another empty bottle. Despite appearing stupid, Sasha almost immediately understood what was going on. Her best friend had a problem. A pill problem.

"Okay, sorry about that. I had just had to place another order on my meds. I'm going crazy right now," Johnson declared as he stepped back into the room. Sasha lifted up all five empty bottles.

"What is this?" she asked. Johnson came by and took all the bottles and threw them back into the oak drawer.

"You know that I'm on Prozac, Sasha, and with everything going on, Dr. Kimp has me taking more," he answered, trying to cover up.

"Oh, I'm sorry," Sasha apologized. She quickly turned back to why she was here. "Johnson, I have to tell you something," she stated strongly.

"Okay, what?" Sasha grabbed Johnson's hand, and they both sat down on one of his couches. She took a deep breath before releasing the floodgates.

"I found out that Emily was sleeping with Talan, so I convinced Lorraine to go out with Faiday so he would break up with Emily, and I've been seeing Jace for a couple weeks now. Nothing big, but I dunno," she said, with her voice almost quivering, full of disgrace. Sasha expected Johnson to say a lot of things, but what he said she didn't imagine. Johnson sighed and then released his floodgate.

"Congrats on you and Jace," Johnson said. "I remember back at the beginning of the year, I was walking down at school when I heard Talan and Emily talking, and he was breaking up with her. It was the day when that story broke about him hooking up with her at the opening of Chic, and during Christmas break, Jen called me and told me that she saw Talan and Lorraine making out," Johnson admitted, remembering he hadn't told Sasha because he got irritated with her and felt like all she cared about was Talan. Sasha was wordless. She knew some part of the story was true, but convinced herself it wasn't. "And," Johnson continued to speak as more memories of Talan's infidelity continued to pour in, "back in Aspen during Thanksgiving break, I saw him and Ashley, that girl we met, kissing when you were gone," he finally disclosed. Sasha got up.

"Oh, my God," she breathed. "Why didn't you tell me!" she exploded.

"I was going to, but then you told me about your dad, and then that's all I thought about, and that's why I'm on Prozac! You've got to tell somebody, Sasha," he said.

"No. We're not turning this around on me. You promised you would not say anything about that—"

"And I'm not," Johnson said, cutting her off.

"I can't deal with this," Sasha lamented as she got her Gucci bag. "You know I would tell you everything," she stated before leaving.

"Sasha, I'm sorry," Johnson yelled after her. It was too late. Sasha had left his house, and probably the clique.

Meanwhile, at Miami's Greynolds Park, Eleanor and Cliff were having a nice picnic enjoying the tranquil setting, which seemed miles away from the noisy, lively city. They were lounging on a soft blanket while Eleanor poured two glasses of very pricey grape juice (since Miss Eleanor didn't drink any beverages with alcohol.)

"What's taking Lily so long?" Cliff asked as Eleanor handed him his drink.

"Not sure," Eleanor replied. "Well, let's just not sit around and mope waiting for her. Have a grape," she suggested. Cliff smiled uneasily. He didn't like just sitting there with Eleanor, alone.

"Thanks for doing this," Cliff said some time later. "Lately it seems that Lily and I only hang out at school."

"No problem."

Talan arrived home after a grueling session with his personal trainer, and all he wanted to do was sleep. But soon enough, he thought about Sasha and felt like he needed to call her and tell her how much he missed her. Karma worked out well for him. He set his gym bag down and flopped onto one of the circular couches in the living room and turned on the mounted plasma TV to ESPN. Christina, the cleaning lady, who he was pretty sure was sleeping with his father, was busy dusting one of the many glass countertops in the condo. Talan's home was the ultimate bachelor pad. Along with a home gym, a killer balcony equipped with a respectable-sized pool, barbeque station, and Jacuzzi, the whole place was furnished with futuristic glass countertops, glass tables, and even a glass wall in the kitchen. The whole place was insipid, with white marble floors, pale fixtures, and white walls. The only things not white were the many awards and trophies of Don Merrick, which were of course displayed in a glass trophy case. With spring break only days away, he was seeing a lot of infomercials on fabo hot spots. He usually went down to Key West and partied it out, but a unique vacation spot states away took his attention (the bit of it that he had), and he was hooked. He got on his phone and called Sasha.

"Hey," she answered like she was a little busy. Probably was with Jace, if you catch the drift.

"I have the best idea for spring break," he stated.

"Oh, really? What?" Sasha replied.

"It's a surprise. But we should all go—Faiday, Lorraine, Johnson—"

"No, not Johnson," she said, cutting him off.

"Why not Johnson?" Talan asked, confused.

"I dunno, but let's not invite him. Listen, I have to go, so I'll text you later," she said hurriedly.

"Okay, love you," he said, with no response.

"Who was it?" Jace asked as Sasha got back in the car.

"Nobody important," Sasha answered as she continued kissing Jace, in his classic vintage Ferrari that she adored so much.

"Sasha . . ." Jace, who was now crutch free, stopped.

"What?" Sasha replied.

"I feel like we hardly get to hang out anymore," he whined. "You're always with Talan."

"He is my boyfriend," she clarified snottily.

"Until how much longer? I'm getting really tired of all this," he admitted, scooting away. Sasha sighed.

"Soon," she repeated, making Jace remember the time before Valentine's when she'd said the same exact thing. Jace nodded and resumed kissing Sasha. He was generally really good in staying within the boundaries Sasha had given him, but today he was getting carried away.

"Jace," Sasha gently pushed him back as he practically lay on top of her.

"Sorry," he apologized as got off her. It was now mid-March, and they had been talking and getting really serious since the start of February. Sasha had never let them get carried away. The most they had ever done were make-outs that were as serious as heart attacks. That's like negative first base for these preps.

"Listen, Jace," Sasha said critically, "the only reason I don't want to rush things is because I didn't wait with Talan, and now look how things have ended up," she disclosed. This was a whole new Sasha. At the beginning of freshman year she was slutty and nice, and now she was deceitful and wouldn't put out.

"I think you should try calling Lily again," Cliff said once more to Eleanor.

"Yeah, this is so unlike her." Eleanor got out her phone and "called" Lily. "No answer again," she stated. "Want some more cheese?"

"No, I'm okay, thanks," Cliff responded, thinking about Lily and how weird it was that she never showed up, when she was so responsible. Soon Eleanor scooted closer to Cliff and fixed his shirt collar. Cliff held his breath as she did, because he felt so uptight.

"You're so tense." Eleanor had caught on. She scooted behind Cliff. "I've been told that I have a wonderful touch," she declared as she started to rub his shoulders and neck. As Eleanor went to work, Cliff managed to get out his phone without Eleanor detecting anything, and soon he saw three texts from Lily asking what he was doing. She texted how upset she was because she had read an article on *Miami Teen Social* on how she was dressed like a tramp at the concert. She thought Eleanor was setting her up for failure. Cliff then reflected on how Eleanor didn't want him using his phone at all. Eleanor soon moved her manicured French tip hands to Cliff's chest and started to nuzzle up against his neck. He quickly got up.

"Hey!" Eleanor snapped as she fell onto the blanket.

"What are you trying to do?" Cliff asked. "I love Lily, and you're trying to start something." He didn't wait for a response. He grabbed his stuff and walked out of the large park. Eleanor took a deep breath and calmly got her cell phone out.

"Mrs. Carrington, it's Eleanor. I have something to tell you, and it's going to be rather hard to hear."

What Eleanor was telling Cynthia Carrington was for sure going to sabotage Lily's relationship with Cliff, and as Lily came home from Cliff's, it would unravel.

"Lily Sophia Carrington, what on earth do you think you're doing?" Cynthia Carrington spoke as Lily walked through the doors of the house.

"What?" Lily asked, surprised.

"You're dating Cliff Bowmen," she established. Lily swallowed. She knew her mom was serious when she saw the vein popping out of her mom's forehead.

"No, no . . . we're just friends. I've told you that over and over." Lily lied, trying to mislead her Ivy League—educated mother.

"You are not permitted to see him again, Lily. Do you understand?" she responded harshly.

"Mom," Lily said, caught off guard.

"Lily!" she said, disciplining her daughter. "It's an embarrassment. You know how humiliated your father would be if he found out that his one and only daughter was dating a meager boy from Overtown?"

"Who told you all this!" Lily screamed, weeping.

"Lily Sophia! What on earth possesses you to speak to your mother like this?" Cynthia exclaimed. Lily cried as she ran to her room. She didn't sleep that whole night. She couldn't even begin to think about Cliff and sadly ignored all his text messages.

As Lily's life seemed to be crumbling down on her, she thought that the only things that mattered to her were disappearing: her boyfriend, her first love (not counting Talan, since that was considered stalking), and her best friend. Little did she know that a girl who was in her class, who seemed totally opposite from her, was having an even worse time.

"Emily." Emily's mom, Miranda, came into her daughter's room. "I'm sorry, but we have to finish paying the, oh . . ." She stopped as she saw Emily lying on her bed appearing to be asleep. Miranda took a piece of her daughter's Tiffany silver jewelry collection, hoping it would be the last thing she would have to sell of her daughter's to pay their mounting debt, but she knew it wouldn't be. Emily understood that she had to sell her nice things to help out her family. The company her dad worked for wasn't doing so well, and as a result, they had to make a huge cut in his salary. Her mom had sold almost every single piece of jewelry she owned, so Emily knew it would be her turn sooner rather than later. She graciously gave her mom her Marc Jacobs boots, Fendi bags, and now genuine Tiffany jewelry to sell. All these items can be found on eBay, by the way, in case you want to help out Emily Parker. In the last couple of months, Emily had lost just about everything. She had already lost her Gucci bag, which she loved to show off, and she was pretty sure her mom had just grabbed her favorite Tiffany bracelet. To make matters worse, she had lost, not one, but two of her boyfriends. One was with her best friend, and the other was with her other best friend. Emily, like Lily, was crying hysterically, not because she had to sell all her nice things, but because she had lost the love of her life. She loved Talan, and he had dumped her twice now. Emily felt hopeless, like her life was over. Emily got up from crying in her dark room and walked to her walk-in closet. There, she retrieved a pistol that she had stashed under her cashmere sweaters, and pulled the gun to the side of her head. Without money she thought she could fall back on Talan, but now without Talan she couldn't fall back on anything. She cried, cherishing the charmed life she once led, but now it was over. She remembered when she skipped a whole night of partying just to go on the Internet and see when this whole recession was going to be over, so she could go back to her old happy life. It only brought up depressing answers. Just as her finger started to feel cold on the handle, she was about to get it over with, when she heard her cell phone buzz with a text in her jean pocket. She set the gun down and got out her phone.

I was thinking that i should bring you and Jen to Hawaii with me. All on me. I wanted to give my friends an awesome spring break☺

The text was from Johnson, and Emily started to cry. Johnson had done so much for her. She put the gun away and fell to floor weeping.

"Emily!" her mom shouted from downstairs. "Charlie's home." Charlie was Emily's older brother who was in college, and she loved him very much.

"Coming!" she sniffled, happy that her brother had come home at a time when they really needed him.

Sabotage can truly ruin someone's life, but in the eyes and minds of the ones sabotaging, what do they really get? Do their lives get any better knowing they have messed up someone else's? Get this, karma is a major bee-otch, and it comes back tenfold. This is *Miami Teen Social*. Have a fun karma-free spring break. Until next time . . .

Chapter Sixteen

Spring Break

Spring break for Hamilton Prep kids is an absolute requirement. Not only does it give time for the whole city of Miami to get detoxified from Hamilton Prep kids' shameless activities, but it also gives the students time to deal with personal issues and let everything out. That, without a doubt, oozes drama, and the more we can fulfill our gossipers' juicy appetites, the more they will log on and buy more issues of *MTS*. The more they buy, the more comfortable *our* spring break is. With that aside, Hamilton Prep kids usually hang around in South Beach, perhaps even Key West if they aren't taking some luxurious trip to Hawaii or Barbados. However, spring break was the last thing on Lily Carrington's mind as she steered her boyfriend, Cliff Bowmen, into an empty classroom.

"Cliff, we can't be together anymore," Lily confessed, crying, to Cliff.

"Why?" he said, panicked as if he scored an F on an algebra paper. She then explained everything.

"For the past week, Eleanor would call me and say that she wanted us to hang, all three of us, but you would never show. Now I understand," Cliff confirmed, saddened.

"Lorena told me that she overheard my mom talking on the phone, and she's making sure we don't speak here at school," Lily informed him, sobbing. Now that's a good way of using the maids.

"So this is the end?" Cliff said with his voice shaking. How sad.

"It can't be—"

"Lily, come on. Your dad is the senator. Whatever he wants goes," Cliff said, heartbroken. Lily remained quiet, knowing that Cliff was right.

If it were up to her parents, they would never allow her to see him again. If they didn't value education so much, they probably would have tried to get Cliff kicked out of Hamilton. It was like a modern-day *Romeo and Juliet.*

"For break, my mom is sending me to this academy camp thing for the musically gifted in Chicago," Lily told him. Cliff nodded, defeated. He hugged Lily closely before going out into the exposure of the hallways, where spies hid and reported to the Carringtons.

"Are you ready, girls?" Johnson asked breathlessly as he walked out of his house and met Jennifer and Emily down by the limo. The girls were accompanied by loads and loads of suitcases. Damn, for how much they packed, one would think that they would be out of Miami for months. No such luck.

"Yeah," Emily said, in high spirits. She was able to come along, thanks to Johnson's broken heart (he was still reeling over the loss of his friendship with Sasha), but more importantly, his bank account. "Thanks for doing all this. You know, paying for everything," she admitted. Johnson twisted his face, confused.

"Okay, it's not like you wouldn't have been able to come if I wasn't paying," he responded, laughing. Emily soon joined him in laughing.

"Why aren't Sasha, Lorraine, and the guys coming?" Jennifer asked as she finished sending some e-mails on her BlackBerry.

"I dunno. They have their boyfriends, and they're doing their thing," Johnson tried to explain, still wishing Sasha was coming along. "Now, all the single whores into the limo!" he cheered as all three hopped into the limo, and they headed off to the airport.

Sasha was packing in her room trying not to think about Johnson, or Jace, or any of the other guys in her life, when she heard someone moving stealthily behind her. She quickly turned around to see Talan.

"God, Talan!" She laughed as she grabbed her chest. "What are you doing here?"

"Nothing. Just thought I would come and help you get packed."

"Oh, well, can you grab my makeup bag in the bathroom?" she asked.

"Nope," Talan replied, smirking. Sasha made a childish face and went into the bathroom to get it herself.

"God, Talan, you're so much help," she joked as she grabbed her kit and walked back into her room. As Sasha was about to put her makeup kit inside her Louis Vuitton suitcase, she noticed a satin jewelry box already inside the suitcase neatly in the center on top of her clothes.

"Talan, what is this?" she asked as she gently picked it up.

"Open it," Talan answered. Sasha opened it, and what met her eyes was a $5,000 pearl necklace.

"Talan, it's so pretty." She intently looked in respect at the beautiful pearls. "Put it on me," she told Talan. As Talan put on the necklace, Sasha almost had to laugh at herself. She had changed Talan. Talan was now the guy that she first started to date. He was caring, and clumsy. She loved when Talan was clumsy. She turned around and stared into Talan's mesmerizing, adorable blue eyes, and was about to cry. She knew she was going to break his heart. It was her mission after all, to get even. One can always throw the nice girl into the lion's den, but her heart will forever hurt when she fights. She quickly changed the subject.

"So where are you taking us?" she asked, wondering.

"It's another surprise," he replied.

"Well, I hope it's as good as this one." She hugged Talan and kissed him.

"We still have quite a while until the plane leaves," Talan informed Sasha, only inches away from her face.

"I know we do," Sasha said as she fell to the bed, still holding Talan.

Hours later, Johnson, Emily, and Jennifer all arrived at the Grand Wailea Resort Hotel and Spa in Wailea, Hawaii, but they were far too exhausted to care about all the champagne and chocolate-drizzled fruit that met them, and went straight into their personal beds and passed out.

Meanwhile, Talan had taken a traditional route in planning spring break, and Sasha and Lorraine were almost mortified as the hot Arizona night hit them. They looked around to see a lake with houseboats. Welcome to Lake Havasu, a place they probably would never have gone to.

"What is this place?" Sasha asked Talan.

"It's Lake Havasu City. Well, this is the lake part of it, anyway," he said as he walked along the dock and managed to find the houseboat he had rented.

"And this is where we will be staying?" Lorraine asked, cringing, not wanting to even step foot inside the houseboat.

"Nothing gets past you, huh, Lorraine?" Talan joked. Lorraine smiled, refraining from reminding him of the time when they were in Mexico and hooked up.

"Looks good to me," Faiday finally said as he walked around the small houseboat and managed to find a bed and slumped into it, dozing off.

"Oh, my God! There's only one bathroom!" Sasha basically shrieked.

"What?" Lorraine freaked as she went into the cramped bathroom. She pulled back the small shower curtain. "I would rather take a shower in the lake than in that. Talan, this place is disgusting," she informed Talan when he appeared in the small hallway.

"I saw it on ESPN; they said it was one of the top vacation spots for spring break," he clarified.

"Maybe, for poor people," Lorraine pouted. "Johnson, Jen, and the E slut went to Hawaii."

"I can give you a plane ticket to join them," Talan joked again as he held Sasha. Lorraine rolled her eyes and exited the packed bathroom.

"I call putting my stuff here first!" Sasha yelled as she saw Lorraine join Faiday.

"We're going to have fun," Talan declared. Sasha smiled as she listened to her boyfriend. With her phone, she texted Jace behind Talan's back (literally).

The next afternoon, after a long morning, Johnson, Emily, and Jennifer were tanning on the sunny beach of Hawaii, before heading off to the spa for some lush, exotic skin treatments.

"God, I love this place. I wish I could stay here forever." Johnson beamed as he reached down for his Mojito.

"I know. This is my second-best vacay spot. First is the south of France." Jennifer laughed as she lounged around on her blanket. As Emily listened, she reflected on the fact that her family could no longer afford to go to the south of France, or even France for anything anymore. She no longer would participate in any of the conversations when it was the season to go to France.

"I wonder what Sasha, Talan, Lorraine, and Faiday are doing," Jennifer said, wondering what was on everyone's mind.

"They're probably in Key West," Johnson answered. Then all of a sudden, like a giant elephant had just appeared on the beautiful beach, Emily shut everyone's mouths with one statement.

"Talan and I were dating earlier, and he just barely broke up with me."

"What?" both Johnson and Jennifer said at the same time.

"Yeah, this is the second time this year," Emily plainly added. Johnson already knew when the first time was.

"What's going on?" Jennifer asked, confused from top to bottom. That led to the discussion that consumed the next thirty minutes of their little lavish vacation. Nothing was left bottled up inside.

"Oh, my God," was all Jennifer could say once Emily had finished.

"I love him," Emily concluded.

"He's not a good guy," Johnson finally spoke. Both Emily and Jennifer stared at Johnson.

"He is," Emily said, almost frustrated. "He's just misunderstood." Johnson sighed and then had his say, telling them everything, all of Talan's betrayals of Sasha.

"Talan has some problems staying faithful, but I know Sasha is cheating on him," Emily said, defending him.

"What? How?" Jennifer asked, not believing her ears. No, not little naive Sasha Chandler.

"Back when we had lunch at Palme D'Or and Sasha came in late, she said she was with Talan. It was obvious that she was doing some X-rated stuff," she said, "but I was with Talan before that, and I know for a fact that he went to the gym right after, because I was texting Faiday, and he said Talan was there."

"Maybe she was doing something else?" Jennifer suggested.

"Why would she lie about it and say she was with Talan then?" Emily asked.

"Jace Costillo," Johnson finally said, more to himself than to them; both Emily's and Jennifer's jaws fell to the ground. They had to remind themselves just how beautiful Sasha was, to believe that she would be able to score with somebody like Jace Costillo. Then, as anticipated, Johnson told them about Sasha's betrayal.

"This is some crazy scheisse!" Jennifer exclaimed. "You're sleeping with Talan, but at the same time you're with Faiday, and Talan is with Sasha, who is sleeping with Jace!" They all took a minute to digest the love pentagon.

The love pentagon was the last thing on Sasha's mind as she watched Talan water-ski right behind the speedboat.

"Babe, you're doing it!" Sasha applauded him, taking a second away from her phone as Talan managed to keep his stance as he water-skied. Last night with the bugs constantly entering the room, and the hot Arizona night, Sasha got hardly any sleep. It wasn't the sleep she was accustomed to. Then again, she was with Talan, and when they were together, sleep was the last thing on either of their minds.

It was a nice day in Lake Havasu, and all the other spring-breakers were swimming, jet-skiing, drinking cold beers, and having a fun time. The Hamilton Prep kids decided that Lake Havasu wasn't that bad, being for "poor" people and all. They, of course, found their own things to entertain themselves with. Boys will be boys, and Faiday was in control of the speedboat as he and Talan competed to see who could impress the girls by doing the coolest stunts and staying the longest on the water skis. After Talan flew off the skis (thanks to Faiday's crazy turns), it was his turn to maneuver the boat, and Faiday's turn on the skis. While the boys competed, Lorraine openly flirted with Talan and Faiday, hugging both of them very sensually. She was, in her words, dressed very casually in a white bikini top and short denim shorts. Sasha was in a similar outfit, but instead of worrying about what was going on with Talan, she used her phone to text Jace, who was with his friends in Key West.

"Maybe next time, eh, Faiday?" Talan joked as he managed to stay longer on the skis, and therefore won.

"Hell, yeah," Faiday replied as they walked back up to the houseboat.

"Okay, we're going on a hike, so put on tennis shoes," Talan informed the girls as he walked into the boathouse.

"Tennis shoes? I didn't bring any," Lorraine complained as she followed him.

"Sasha, can I talk to you?" Faiday asked once Talan and Lorraine went inside.

"Yeah," she replied as they walked around the boathouse, pretending to look at the lake.

"I think I want to get back together with Emily," Faiday disclosed.

"What!? Are you insane?" Sasha exclaimed, ridiculing him. They looked around to see if Talan or Lorraine had noticed that they were talking in secret.

"I like her more than I like Lorraine, and you pressured me all kinds to dump Emily and go for Lorraine. Besides, Lorraine is annoying," he explained.

"Oh, my God, Faiday. I have something going on, and you're not going to mess it up! Do you get that?" Sasha questioned angrily as she turned around and left.

"So, is that a yes?" Faiday called out, scratching his jet-black hair. "Can I dump her?"

While Sasha and Faiday ate bologna sandwiches and, behind closed doors, gave each other relaxing massages (maybe Sasha was doing a little convincing about staying with Lorraine?), Talan got dressed in another room and Lorraine did some sunbathing. Back in Hawaii, Johnson, Emily, and Jennifer were getting private massages from expert masseurs.

"What's on your mind, Johnson?" Emily asked the very quiet Johnson.

"Everything," he replied. Boy, this just ruined his vacation, didn't it? It came across as if all Johnson had been thinking about was the love pentagon. Is he upset that he wasn't part of it? Wouldn't that be something—a love six-figure-gon, or whatever it's called.

Even though it was sunny and fun in Hawaii and Lake Havasu, back in Miami it was gloomy and rainy. Cliff was at home watching TV in sweats, bored out of his mind. He thought about Lily and couldn't even consider seeing her at school, and not being able to say a straightforward "hi," because her parents disliked him. They liked him just fine when they thought they were close friends, but Eleanor Vanderthorn had destroyed a growing relationship. Lily was now on her way to Chicago to attend an academy that Cliff really hoped she would take full advantage of. There was an unexpected knock at his door. Not only was it a bit stormy, but it was late. Cliff stood up, stretched, and answered it.

"Lily!" He couldn't believe it. Standing right in front of him, was a very soaked Lily Carrington.

"I'm sorry, but I couldn't do it," she said. "Getting on that plane was going to be a mistake. I love you, Cliff. You make my life mean something. You taught me that there is more to high school than reading and getting good grades," she declared as if she were proposing right on the spot.

"I love you, too," Cliff said as he rushed to Lily and held her in his arms. Lily and Cliff hugged tightly through the entire night. It all happened so fast. How will they continue their relationship? (Sneaking around the senator is not easy.) If people like Talan Merrick and Lorraine

Everly get to be with the ones they like, then why shouldn't Lily and Cliff? Best wishes to them.

Back at Lake Havasu, the little hike that Talan had planned was not going well. He was tired of hearing Lorraine complain because she was wearing flip-flops and her expensive pedicure was getting ruined. Sasha wouldn't stop texting, and Talan had kinda led them off the trail. He was hoping to have the benefit of bonding with Sasha (when she wasn't texting). Lorraine had gotten tired, and she was riding on Faiday's back a little behind Sasha and Talan. The trail, to a certain degree, was a unique one. During the hike, they had seen everything from sand dunes, to rugged canyons, basins, tall cacti (Sasha and Lorraine spent ten minutes arguing if it was a tree or a flower), and assorted flora and fauna. They had seen a coyote, and Sasha thought it was a dog; unfortunately, it was scared away, so it couldn't have bitten any of the Hamilton Prep kids and given them rabies.

"Who are you texting?" Talan finally asked lightheartedly as Sasha refused to look away from her phone.

"Nobody," she replied.

"Oh, really?" Talan said as he snatched the phone up and jogged ahead of Sasha.

"Talan!" she cried out. Was Sasha scared that Talan might be able to read any of the messages? What would he find? We know! Talan turned and dangled the phone above Sasha's head.

"Come on. Get it, Sasha," he teased.

"Talan, please," Sasha replied seriously.

"All right." Talan gave her back the phone. "I see who you like more."

"Talan," Sasha whined as she hooked her arm inside of Talan's and leaned against him. Talan smiled and kissed her forehead.

As night fell back in Hawaii, it was time to go clubbing. Emily was finishing putting on satin yellow peep-toe pumps, to flatter her flame-red

Burberry tiered tank dress. Jennifer was wearing a black-and-white print sheath dress from Michael Kors, and Johnson had just finished taking three of his happy pills. Yikes! He was ready to go out tonight, to release himself.

While Johnson, Emily, and Jennifer did what Sasha, Talan, Lorraine, and Faiday wished they could do, they were unfortunately (well, maybe it's fortunately) lost in the wilderness, and it was dark.

"I can't believe this, Talan," Sasha sulked as she rode on Talan's back, worn-out from walking.

"Sorry, babe, but I guess we must have gotten off the trail," Talan concluded as he stopped. Faiday and Lorraine soon caught up.

"So, what are we doing?" Faiday asked as Lorraine got off his back. (He quietly thanked God. Lorraine was a bit heavier than what he was used to carrying.)

"I don't know; the trail is somewhere around here," Talan guessed, tired and hungry.

"It's so dark out here," Lorraine nagged while slapping mosquitoes away. (Please give her West Nile.) Everyone, including Faiday, rolled his or her eyes, so drained from hearing her voice. Lorraine had been endlessly complaining for the last hour. Through the trees, Talan spotted a massive bonfire on a clearing.

"What the hell is going on over there?" he asked as they walked toward the trees.

"Maybe they know a way out of here and back to the lake?" Sasha suggested. Just then, possibly, they heard the scariest screams (no clever remark intended) they had ever heard.

"Please don't kill us!" a girl bawled. The eyes of all four of them widened in horror. What they saw in the clearing was a huge bonfire, massive, and around it were a couple men almost dancing around the fire. Next to the fire was the most disturbing thing of all—a couple tied up.

"What . . . what is this?" Talan stammered, not finding the right words to say.

"Oh, my God," Lorraine muttered softly, horror-stricken. All four stood there, Sasha and Lorraine in skimpy bikini tops and short denim shorts, Talan and Faiday in tank tops and board shorts . . . all four could die without a hint of designer clothes!

"Please! Please!" they heard the guy yell.

"I'm not watching this; I'm leaving and getting someone!" Lorraine hissed, extremely disturbed by the whole situation. After that, a very clichéd thing happened—one that people think happens only in the movies—and as Lorraine turned around she stepped on a twig and it loudly snapped, almost echoing throughout the whole surrounding area.

"My foot!" Lorraine cried as she grabbed her foot, which had been penetrated by the twig straight through the flip-flop. Talan quickly looked back at the bonfire as Sasha went down to shut up Lorraine. The strange men, hearing what had happened, soon starting shining rather large flashlight beams through the trees and shrubbery, looking for intruders.

"You've got to be quiet," Sasha whispered as she covered Lorraine's mouth. Lorraine fell to the ground, crying.

"Shut up, Lorraine," Faiday commanded as he came down to the trail and knelt beside Lorraine. "I know your foot hurts, but you have to shut up, or else they'll hear us," he tried to explain. Sasha quietly joined Talan, who was still ducking from the beams.

"We have to get out of here," Talan stated. He was breathing irregularly, his heart just about beating out of his tanned chest. Sasha nodded, but in yet another horror movie cliché, Sasha's phone started to blink on and off, signaling her phone was dying.

"Over there!" they heard one of the guys bark. Oh, crap.

"Run!" Talan demanded as he grabbed Sasha's hand. Faiday quickly helped Lorraine up.

"You have to run, okay?" Faiday said sternly. Lorraine nodded, but her foot was bleeding and there was no serious chance she was going to run. (For God's sake, rather than thinking she could be tortured to death, and have her remains thrown into a bonfire, she was thinking how bad her feet were going to look in heels with a big scar on them.) Then she looked in the distance and noticed two headlights.

"Wait! Oh, my God, help." Lorraine stumbled as she detached herself from Faiday and started hopping toward the truck.

"Lorraine! No!" Faiday angrily said.

"It's help!" Lorraine cried. "Help us! Please!" she screamed and waved at the truck that was approaching the clearing, like she had just escaped from an asylum. As Lorraine continued to hop, she stopped dead in her tracks. To her utter shock, the men who were torturing the couple had stopped and flagged down the truck. Lorraine almost passed out when she saw the men point toward her, and the truck fueled on towards her. Lorraine shook her head, pleading and crying, but all of a sudden she grew some Wonder Woman powers and dove in between some trees just as the truck approached her. Her landing wasn't lovely, and she tumbled down the hill, hitting rocks and shrubs, and then finally, the hard ground.

"Where's Lorraine and Faiday?" Sasha asked, out of breath as she and Talan stopped running.

"I don't know," Talan confessed. Talan looked around and soon spotted a light down the trail. "Look."

"It's a house!" Sasha exclaimed as she started running toward it.

As they reached the light, they saw a small cabin, with two Broncos parked outside. To their relief, the Broncos had police lights on them, and seals on the doors.

"The police," Sasha breathed. She and Talan burst inside the cabin and made the game wardens' night, as well as ours.

"Okay, calm down, Miss," one of the game wardens told Sasha as she recited her story rather loudly.

"Our friends are out there, and you guys are still asking me questions. They could be dead!" Sasha yelled again. The female officer took a deep breath to relax herself from the young spring-breaker, who was getting on her last nerve with her constant yelling. Doesn't Sasha know what an indoor voice is? The other officer had taken Talan into a room and was asking Talan questions.

"No, why would we be lying?" Talan demanded, irritated.

"I'm not saying you're lying," the male officer said, "but we get a lot of kids, especially this time of the year, coming around the cabin and vandalizing everything, telling us exaggerated stories about how their friends are out there lost," he explained. Talan buried his face into the palms of his hands, frustrated with the officer. "They usually are high on drugs, or have drank way too much."

"My dad is Don Merrick—he used to play for the Miami Dolphins—and if you don't get your ass on the phone and call the real police, not the animal police or whatever the hell you are, I'm going to get him down here and . . ." Talan was so frustrated he didn't even know what to say or how to finish his sentence.

"Hank," the woman warden said as she peered through the door.

"Yeah," Hank replied.

"The Devil's Cannibals are back in town," she reported. Talan's head popped up. Hank sighed, annoyed, and they soon reunited Sasha and Talan and told them about The Devil's Cannibals.

"They're just a bunch of weirdos who go out in the desert and perform these . . . Satanic rituals. In order to be a member, you have to pretend to get sacrificed into the bonfire to the devil or something like that," Hank explained, sounding extremely irritated by the whole situation.

"So your friends are okay. They're probably lost, but we've talked to Sid, the supposed cult leader, or whatever you want to call him, and we've told him over and over to stop doing the rituals here," the woman warden told them.

"You guys aren't the only ones that bust in here with the story about a big bonfire, and people screaming," Hank added.

"We'll go out looking for your friends, and everything will be back to normal, and you can enjoy the rest of your spring break," the woman warden, Tracy, said. Sasha leaned into Talan and sighed. This night was one of the wildest nights of her life! That includes the night when she had to bounce back between Talan and Jace. Sasha didn't think it could get wilder than that.

Hank took Sasha and Talan back to the boathouse.

"I'm so scared, Talan," Sasha confessed as she turned on the shower.

"Don't be," Talan said to comfort her. "They said that those people were just some losers who did retarded devil crap." He hugged his girlfriend. Sasha flashed back to when Talan had grabbed her hand and basically dragged her away from the situation. Even though it wasn't anything now, she remembered how Lorraine and Faiday argued. She thought about her old self and how she was right when she said that she and Talan were something special.

After taking a quick shower to wash off the sweat and outdoor smell, Sasha found Talan talking to Hank outside the boathouse.

"They found your friends. They're okay," Hank was telling Talan. "The girl is pretty banged up—she fell down a small hill—but the boy is fine."

"Thank God," Sasha said as she came into view. Talan wrapped his arm around her. Sasha, for a second, had thought she had lost one of her friends, and then she remembered that she did lose a couple of her friends, Johnson and Emily. She felt so bad for putting Johnson in a situation that ultimately made him a Prozac addict.

The following day, back in Hawaii, having no idea what their friends had just gone through, Johnson, Emily, and Jennifer were all playing tennis at the resort. They had just had a fabulous breakfast. (Extremely late, though. They were out clubbing until two in the morning, and woke up at eleven.)

"Damn it," Johnson cursed as he missed the ball.

"Where's your A game?" Emily questioned, as she had won yet another game against Johnson.

"I dunno," Johnson replied, yawning.

"Are you still tired from last night?" Jennifer asked from the sidelines.

"I dunno," Johnson repeated, extremely confused. Well, Johnson, my dear, mixing alcohol with antidepressants is not only stupid, but just cancels out all the effects that Prozac is supposed to have. Johnson is depressed once again. Maybe a phone call will cheer him up?

"Hold on," Johnson said as he went to answer his ringing cell phone. "What?" he asked as he saw it was Sasha calling.

"Hello?" he answered, not sure what to think, let alone say.

"Johnson, it's me, Sasha." Duh.

"Yeah," Johnson responded.

"I'm so sorry for everything I did and caused. I want all of us to be friends again. I'm so confused right now, and I need you," Sasha blurted out like she was in a confessional with her priest.

"I feel really bad, too," Johnson agreed with a hint of happiness in his voice.

"Before you say anything else," Sasha added, "I've got one heck of a story to tell you."

Spring break is usually a time to get a nice tan and enjoy the time you have with your friends. As much as the Hamilton Prep kids might have deserved having their break ruined, there is no funny line between life and death. Don't get killed. *Miami Teen Social . . .*

Chapter Seventeen

Out in the Open

Spring break is over, but as Hamilton Prep students start coming back, no one has any idea of the scandal that is about to erupt. Sasha, Talan, Johnson, and the others expect everyone will be talking about their near-death experience, but sadly for them, one article circulates around the entire school right on the morning they are welcomed back to the school.

"OMG! Boy, do we have a story to tell. Talsha (we haven't used that name in quite a while) have been up to some things. Get ready, hospital, with your STD kits, and get ready, fellow readers, with your savory appetite for wild preps. We have reported on Talan's cheatings in the past with Sasha's best friends, Emily Parker and Lorraine Loosely Everly, but now get ready for Sasha's. But first, reports say that little Talan didn't end things with Emily Parker like everyone else thought he did. A couple months after breaking it off, they secretly got back together. But don't feel bad for Sasha, because she had her own little fun. While Talan and Emily were together (FYI, Emily was still with Faiday Hayward, Talan's best friend, at the time), Sasha was with Hamilton Prep junior Jace Costillo! Yes, OMG. So for all of you who don't get it, Talan was dating Sasha, but he was sneaking around with Emily, who was with Faiday, who later dumped Emily for her

159

and Sasha's friend Lorraine, who had hooked up with Talan in Mexico months ago, but at the same time that Sasha was with Jace Costillo. See, we knew that Sasha was more like her mother than she was letting on."

Comments~

Ray34 says—That school is like a brothel. Everyone hooks up with everyone! I can't believe it. That's the true meaning of friends with benefits.

Yuri<3HP says—I can't believe Sasha Chandler landed two of HP's hottest guys. And Talan got back together with his best friend's girl. That's insane.

"What is this?" Sasha panicked as she read the article that everyone was talking about. She looked at Talan next to her, who stood planted down like a statue. The whole school was looking at her and Talan.

"Emily, what the hell?" Faiday freaked as he questioned his ex-girlfriend, who had allegedly cheated on him with his best friend—again. The first time Faiday let it slide because it was just speculation, but now he knew it was true. Everyone in the whole entire school was reading it, and he was humiliated.

"Faiday, calm down," Emily said, trying to soothe her very furious ex-ex-boyfriend. Faiday snarled and looked down the hallway. "No, Faiday," Emily said, holding her ex-boyfriend back. Faiday marched straight up to his supposed best friend, (hold your breath) and punched Talan right in his jaw. Talan hit the lockers. Damn, even when he gets punched in the face, Talan somehow still makes it look good.

"What is wrong with you?" Faiday yelled as Emily and a couple of the other guys held him back. Sasha stood in horror at everything that was happening. All hell was breaking loose. As people calmed Faiday down,

Talan immediately got up, but instead of fighting back with Faiday, he turned to Sasha.

"Is it true?" he asked. Sasha was taken aback by his tranquility.

"Yeah," she admitted, "but it was before I knew how much you cared about me. I found Emily's bracelet in your room, and all the other stories . . ."

"I know"—Talan stopped—"and it's okay. I forgive you."

"What?" Sasha said. Talan put his arms around Sasha and hugged her. As he did, they saw Jace at the end of the hallway. For a second they both looked at him, and then Talan hugged Sasha closer. Sasha closed her eyes, unable to look at either Jace or Talan.

Lily was oblivious or simply didn't care about her classmates' doings. She was walking up to Eleanor Vanderthorn, the girl who had single-handedly destroyed her first actual relationship. Lily showed that she did have some wild prep in her. She spent the whole break at Cliff's apartment. She called the academy she was supposed to be staying at and pretended to be her mom saying that her daughter's flight had been canceled and she was so sorry that she couldn't make it. Bad, we know.

"Next time you to try to steal my boyfriend, I'll . . . You'll be sorry," Lily stated. Eleanor rolled her eyes.

"Oh, Lil," Eleanor pouted, "he came on to me, so I had to call your mother and inform her of the barbarian you were secretly dating. How was Chicago?" she asked, smirking.

"Lovely," Lily responded. "You're a manipulative, deceitful, sad girl who gets pleasure at seeing others hurt," Lily strongly informed her once good friend.

"Ouch, does this mean we're not going to be partners for student council? How on earth will you win without me?" Eleanor asked.

"I will win without you," Lily confirmed as she turned around. "You don't have my vote, and please tell your boyfriend to stop texting me," she said loudly so Eleanor's group of friends could hear. Eleanor turned red in the face, and yelled as she walked away.

The day was nearly done. Talan and Faiday had managed to not get into any altercations. Faiday had broken up with Lorraine, who cried out openly, trying to make things about her, but nobody, other than her friends, cared (and even they couldn't take her drama).

"What are you going to do now?" Johnson asked Sasha as they walked through the quad.

"I'm not sure, and I can't believe this got out," Sasha explained. "Who would do this? Who would know all of that?" Sasha continued to question.

"I dunno," Johnson mumbled, "but putting that aside, you can't continue seeing both Talan and Jace, no matter how hot they are."

"I know. I love Talan, but I can't let go of Jace," Sasha grumbled, ready to pull her extensions out. "I was on a mission to ruin Talan to make him pay for cheating on me, but when I saw how much he cared for me, I started having second thoughts." Sasha clarified, "What happened over break just put everything into perspective for me. I need to love my friends and my mom more. It's just so much more complicated."

"Sasha," Johnson said, "I know what it feels like to have a mom who doesn't give a crap, but you guys are all each other has."

"I just need to get things in order."

"Here." Johnson stopped her. He got a small piece of paper and jotted down a phone number.

"What is this?" Sasha asked as she took the slip of paper.

"Her name is Julie Kimp, and she's my therapist." Johnson laughed. "You should talk to her."

After school, Sasha secretly sneaked out of Talan's sight as he talked to a couple of his friends.

"Jace," Sasha called out as Jace practiced football with a couple of his friends at the football field. He walked over, all gloomy.

"Hey," she awkwardly greeted him.

"It's time," he said sternly.

"For what?" Sasha asked, knowing exactly what he was talking about.

"It's either me or him, Sasha."

"Please, don't make me choose right now," Sasha whispered, tearing up.

"You have to make up your mind sooner or later," Jace concluded as he walked away. Sasha cried as she turned around. Her whole life was shattering. She looked into her Chanel clutch and pulled out a slip of a paper. She dialed the number on her cell phone.

"Julie Kimp, please."

Being the genius that she was, Lily had found a way to still spend time with Cliff. (Even though it was with a whole bunch of their friends, and it was at times relatively boring.) Lily was at her friend Bernice's, and they were having a book club meeting. Bernice had a whole loft to herself at her family's condo in Brickell. Lily was contentedly reading *Invisible Man* by Ralph Ellison. She was leaning against Cliff, who smiled as he read. She loved it. She wondered how Cliff felt when he read the book. In the book the narrator felt socially invisible, and Cliff probably felt like that too, sitting in a condo as big as his whole apartment complex, and having the senator's wife basically say he wasn't good enough for their daughter. Her parents thought she was miles away from Cliff and his bad neighborhood, when in actuality she was leaning against him reading a good book, all the while still having a fantastic view of the financial district of Miami.

"Ms. Carrington," Hilda, Bernice's maid, silently called. Lily looked up from looking at Cliff. "It's your mother." She glanced at Cliff, but Cliff seemed to be in another world that Ralph Ellison had created.

"Can you tell her I will call her back when we are done with reading time," Lily stated as she got back to her book.

A week later, Sasha Chandler found herself face-to-face with therapist Julie Kimp, and as soon as Sasha said hello they started to make progress. Sasha was dressed demurely in a gray tweed skirt, a blazer, and the nice pearl necklace that Talan had bought her. Her hair was neatly tucked back.

"I wish I could talk to my mom, but it's just so . . . easier said than done," Sasha said. Julie was furiously jotting down notes.

"Why do you feel like you can't?" Julie asked.

"My mom is more like a child than an adult," Sasha confessed. That statement was true. Lenny Chandler was still vacationing with some guys out of town.

"Well, why don't you do something that you would usually do with your friends but with your mother instead?" Julie suggested. "It would be a good bonding experience."

"Maybe," Sasha said, now eager to focus on Talan and Jace.

Exactly one week later, Sasha found herself running out of time, and Jace was even ignoring her text messages. She was yet again on Dr. Kimp's sofa, blurting out how she felt.

"I really like Jace, but during spring break and even before that, Talan was becoming the boy that I fell in love with at the beginning of the year," Sasha professed. "I don't know who to pick. It's like I'm on *The Bachelorette* or something." Julie laughed and then said something that made Sasha say, "What?"

"How about neither?" Julie repeated. Sasha looked at Julie as if she were the one who needed shrinking. "You need to get your closest relationships mended first. And that would be your relationship with your mother. Without all these boys in your life, you and your mom can fully concentrate on just you guys and be open and honest with each other." Julie stopped, letting Sasha digest everything. Sasha soon nodded her head.

"I think you're right." She smiled. "If they truly love me, then they will understand."

"That's right," Julie finished as she looked at her watch. "Well, my next client should be here, so see you next week."

"Okay," Sasha said as she got her bag. "Johnson was right. You are good."

"Sinclair?" Julie asked.

"Yeah, he recommended you. Don't you see him every week?"

"He stopped seeing me a while back."

"I guess he is seeing another therapist. I'll see you later." Sasha exited the room, leaving a very concerned Julie Kimp.

Sasha and Johnson were on the beach enjoying the weekend and working on their tans, but more importantly talking about Sasha's new priorities and plans for her "new life."

"But yeah, I think that's what I'm going to do," Sasha informed the heir, so content about it, as they lay on their towels on the warm beach, which was frolicking with children, seagulls, and adults.

"I think it's a good idea. I applaud you on what you're doing." Johnson smiled. Not one second after he finished his sentence the subject came up . . . again. "I'm sorry for bringing this up, but how *Miami Teen Social* got their stories is still bothering me at night. I feel like my whole house is bugged or something." Sasha laughed and then quickly turned serious.

"How they get their stories are by lowlifes who have nothing better to do than to make our lives miserable and air all of our dirty laundry," she answered as she flipped onto her front, trying to get her back tanned. Johnson thought for a second, and as he did it was as if a lightbulb went off in his head.

"Hold on," Johnson said, trying to piece everything together. "Everything that was 'leaked' was something that only someone who was in it would know." He stopped for a minute thinking about it and leaned up, and soon Sasha joined him, thinking about it too. The way they thought resembled two seniors planning a prank—one couldn't believe they were actually taking time out to think, but they did make progress.

"Or someone who knew what was going on the whole time, but maybe wasn't in it," Sasha finished. "Oh, my God, it had to be one of our friends. Someone on the scene."

"I think I know who," Johnson finished.

"Hey, what's up, guys?" Jennifer greeted them as she met with Sasha and Johnson at Johnson's house. Johnson and Sasha were somberly sitting on his bed until Johnson simply walked up to Jennifer and gave her printed articles from the *Miami Teen Social* website. "What is this?" Jennifer asked. She stopped once she came to grips with what they were. They were articles about the rumors Johnson was on drugs, and how he got his heart broken by a waiter in Aspen, Talan's fling with Lorraine in Mexico, Johnson being on Prozac, and the love pentagon—all the stories *she* had leaked to *Miami Teen Social*.

"I'm so sorry," Jennifer mumbled, having been discovered. Johnson's heart ached seeing his once great friend in tears, but then he remembered all embarrassment he had to undergo once the whole school found out he was on antidepressants. Wonder how they would feel if they found out he was addicted to them?

"Why, Jen?" Sasha asked, standing up, frustrated. Sasha could understand Lorraine doing it, or even Emily, but never Jen. Jennifer took a deep, muffled breath.

"When Trevor left, I started hanging around a lot with his cousin's boyfriend, and he worked for *Miami Teen Social*, and said I could probably be featured a lot in it if I would leak out stories to them about my friends, and so I did." Jennifer started to cry hysterically, "I'm sorry. I didn't think the stories were going to be much, but being with him was as if I still had a piece of Trevor here with me. That's why I did it."

"Jennifer," Johnson spoke softly, trying to comfort her.

"No, I'm sorry," Jennifer quickly apologized again before running out of the room. Johnson and Sasha looked at each other, and both quickly felt filled with remorse and guilt.

That Monday with the weekend over, Sasha was getting ready in Johnson's bathroom for school. She was straightening her hair when her phone buzzed. She was surprised by whom the text was from

"Jennifer."

I no I'm probably the last person u wanted to talk 2. But I wanted u 2 no that I will not be returning to Hamilton for the rest of the school year. I told my parents everything, and they r sending me 2 my aunts in Atlanta for the rest of the school year & they said I could stay

with Trevor for the whole summer if I behaved at my aunts. So I guess one good thing did come out of this for me. I am so sorry for all the hurt I caused. I hope to see you some time in August. Jen.

"Johnson," Sasha called, "I got this text from . . ."

"Jennifer," he filled in while standing by the doorway. "Yeah, me too." If it weren't for the extra Prozac he was taking, Johnson probably would have felt extremely sad about losing a good friend.

Jennifer Henderson has exited the building. So we will just have to resort to other methods in getting our stories, huh? Despite her departure, we are sure that the drama will still reign free regardless of the cheery mood everyone else at Hamilton is in with school coming to a close. We always find ways. *Miami Teen Social . . .*

Chapter Eighteen

Decisions

Student council elections were just minutes away, and Lily was backstage taking long, calming breaths. She would soon have to recite her speech, which Cliff had helped her with, and hope that she could sway the vote against the other four students running for secretary. In the audience a clique of freshmen were still talking about what their friend had done. Well, just mainly one girl was.

"I can't believe Jennifer," Lorraine continued nagging. She was sitting next to a very uninterested Emily, who was about to scream at Lorraine if she didn't shut up. "She's such a bitch. She did that thing on the wall, and this whole time we thought it was Lily. She left and isn't coming back for the whole summer. She is so scared we'll tear her up. But I don't care enough about her to do that." Johnson overheard Lorraine and rolled his eyes.

"I know this sounds crazy, but I understand where Jennifer was coming from," Johnson whispered to Sasha.

"In a way I'm happy too, that she did leak everything out, because now I can't hide from it anymore and I have to deal with it," Sasha disclosed, glancing toward Talan, who was seated a couple rows ahead of her with his friends. He looked back and smiled at her. A small pain made its way into Sasha's stomach as she smiled back. She knew she would have to follow the advice of her therapist and break up with him soon.

"I just wish she didn't have to move," Johnson confessed. "She was always here for me."

"Her parents are letting her stay with Trevor for the whole summer. I'm pretty sure that's what she wanted," Sasha explained.

"Yeah," Johnson added, "I didn't want things to end like this, though." He looked at Sasha, and they both rested their heads against one another as student council speeches commenced. Emily then soon turned to Johnson, who was sitting next to her, and leaned against him, while Lorraine turned to her left and continued to denigrate Jennifer with her friend Hannah.

"I don't know how much more I can take of Lorraine," Emily confessed, laughing quietly. Both Johnson and Sasha nodded their heads in agreement.

"Lily Carrington," Eleanor said backstage, "you're up." Lily hearing her simply ignored her and got her note cards and organized them.

"Break a leg, and you can always try out again next year," Eleanor continued. "You know, when I'm not here."

"Whatever," Lily said as she walked out onto the stage. The faces of all the Hamilton Prep students met her, and she suddenly became nervous. Her mother and Cliff were out there—the only two people she cared about. She took a deep breath before starting.

"Good afternoon. I'm Lily Carrington, and I will be a sophomore next year. I am currently the freshman class president. I am standing here for all the students who would like a change in this environment. Whether it's a simple change like perhaps wanting to adjust the way the student lounge works, or a more significant change, such as how the discipline acts are handled. That's why I would like to be a part of student council, so I can bring order to and become more effective in dealing with the issues we face as teens in school today. I would have a bigger platform to openly discuss issues that my friends and I have personally dealt with. Not only have I been a 4.0 student all this year, but I have organized fun bonfires for my class, and managed to go out to social events and praise Hamilton Prep for their wonderful curriculum. My mind will always be open for anybody who has suggestions. If voted in, this summer I will set up a webpage wherein you can anonymously display and e-mail any problems that you may be facing involving Hamilton students or its campus. Thank you so much." Students, faculty, and parents applauded, and Lily exited the stage all high and mighty. On her way out, she passed a very sour-looking Eleanor.

"Hey, Talan," Sasha said a bit awkwardly as she arrived at his condo after school.

"Hey," he replied as he turned off the TV and walked up to her. "What's up?" Sasha straightforwardly reached into her Marc Jacobs bag and handed him a small pink box.

"What is this?" Talan said rhetorically as he opened it. He sighed once he saw that it was the ring and pearl necklace he had given her. "I don't get it."

"Talan," she started to explain, "the school year is almost out, and I want us to be able to concentrate on different things in our lives. You have your football that you're going to practicing for all summer long. You're going to make varsity," she more or less congratulated him, "and I want to start connecting more with my mother. It's not going to be fair if we become selfish and just throw everything else aside because we want to make it as a couple." Talan looked at Sasha, and slowly started nodding his head, almost comprehending what she was saying. "We had a good run," Sasha added, "nine wonderful months. The longest relationship I have ever had."

"I know," Talan said, smirking. "Come on," he said as he hugged her and led her to the doorway. The two hugged and parted on terms of being great friends.

Lily had just returned from another book club meeting at Bernice's, in which she and Cliff celebrated Lily's amazing speech, but the celebratory spirit was about to crash and burn thanks to another Jennifer—but in the form of a geek.

"I am not going to get your father involved in this, because this is over," Cynthia informed her bitterly as she sat in Lily's sitting room waiting for her daughter to come home.

"What are you talking about?" Lily asked, with her heart beating frantically.

"I told you that you were not permitted to speak to Cliff again, and now I find out that you are sneaking around with him." Cynthia arose from her seat and walked to Lily. (More like glided. Poor Lil was so frightened, she practically fell into a chair, and remained there.) Lily knew that someone had told her about the book club. Lily started to cry, knowing her second shot was . . . well, shot.

"You are no longer to ever see him, Lily, and if you do, I will have no other choice but to call Headmaster Trimble and tell him to please relocate Cliff Bowmen to another more suitable school . . . and trust me, he will." Lily thought that all the damage that her mother could inflict on her had already been done, but we already know how Lily's luck is. "This summer we are joining your dad at our DC home, and we are leaving the day after school lets out. We will return in August, when, hopefully, you have all this rebellious attitude out of you." Lily remained frozen with the exception of the tears streaming down her cheeks. "Now, Lily, please don't cry. It's for the best. Get ready. We're having dinner with the Masons, and I want to tell them how well your speech went," Cynthia told her, wiping her daughter's cheek.

It looked as if one heartache after another was still to come. Sasha was at the Miami Beach pier waiting for Jace. She looked out into the setting sun. Her mother would be home soon, and she wanted nothing other than to see her face when she got home. She knew she was doing the right thing.

"Sasha." Jace broke the image of her mother from Sasha's mind. She turned around to see Jace standing with his hands in his pockets. He was wearing his varsity football jacket, which Sasha loved, and a backward cap.

"Thanks for coming." It wasn't easy for Sasha to get Jace to come, but he was here, and now she had to break his heart.

"I love you, Jace, but we can't be together right now," she started. Jace looked down and then back up at the sun, not understanding. "I don't feel good here, Jace," Sasha soon said as she walked closer to him and brought his hand up to her heart. Sasha was teary-eyed, but she had promised Johnson that she wasn't going to cry. "I have to fix this before I can be happy, and right now the only person that can fix this is my mom, and I'm going crazy right now just thinking about talking to her." Sasha couldn't finish the sentence, because Jace wrapped his arms around her and the two hugged. Sasha took a deep breath, knowing things were going to be okay with Jace. He understood.

"I'll always be here for you, Sasha," Jace whispered. If it seemed complicated for Sasha, well, it was nearly impossible for Jace to let her do what she needed to do.

"I did it." Sasha walked into Johnson's room, looking like a disarrayed hot mess . . . on the outside anyway. Johnson could tell right away that his best friend—who had been through the wringer this year with fights and makeups with Talan, friends giving her the cold shoulder, being in that house of hers all alone with those horrible memories, and the loss and the regaining of her best friend—was a healthier soul on the inside now.

"I'm so proud of you, Sasha." Johnson gave Sasha a hug, and despite being strong with the other guys, Sasha broke down in the arms of Johnson.

"Can I stay the night? I don't want to be alone," she cried softly.

"Yes, of course."

The following day at school, hallways were vacant; students were in small groups in classrooms, the quad, or the auditorium mingling, saying farewells, and wishing a fun summer vacation to all. Lily was in one of the classrooms with her friends Bernice Anderson and Charlie Feeney.

"This summer my parents are taking me to the French Riviera," Bernice declared with a full-on metal mouth. Braces without a doubt were not for her. Lily wasn't paying much attention to the conversation as she feverishly wrote down all her feelings to Cliff in a farewell letter. She wasn't breaking things off, but was saying that her mom knew everything. She warned him that if they got back together her mom would remove him from the school. The last thing she wrote was, "You are and always will be my first love, Love, Lily." What a touching letter.

"Attention, students," Headmaster Trimble's voice spoke over the intercom, "the votes are in, and here are the results for next year's student council. For treasurer it's Jeremy Latka. Secretary is Lily Carrington."

"Oh, my God, Lil. Congratulations." Bernice hugged her friend, and Lily tried to show a humble attitude for her triumph, but the one thing she wanted was slipping away from her. She had nothing to look forward to next year.

"Vice president is Matt Kaiser, and next year's president is Eleanor Vanderthorn. Congratulations to all who made it. All the class reps will be the same except for the freshman class, who have voted for Hannah Reynolds and Ashton Cross. Now . . ." Headmaster Trimble went into a spew about summer and next year.

"I can't believe Hannah and Ashton got in," Bernice whined.

"Why, they're in the 'in' crowd. They're popular," Charlie pointed out.

"But they're not even interested in student council," Bernice countered. Bernice was a little bitter she didn't get in. "What are they going to share at the meetings? How hungover they are?"

Meanwhile, out in the halls Johnson was telling the girls all about his plan for summer.

"We should all rent a house in the Hamptons. I've read everywhere it is the 'it' place to go for the summer," he said, not being able contain himself—he was basically jumping up and down, full of excitement.

"Sounds so awesome! Yay! I'm so proud of Hannah, though, but I totally love the idea," Lorraine chipped in. Johnson shook his head in dislike of Hannah, and turned to Emily and Sasha. As he looked at Sasha, she gave him a look saying, sorry, but you know what's going on. Johnson nodded and looked at Emily.

"I already talked to this agent girl. She and Sasha helped me pick out the most fabulous mansion. It's a bit pricey to rent out. She said it was going to be about $120,000 for the three months, but it's well worth it."

"Wow, that's a lot," Emily pointed out, almost out of breath.

"I'll chip in my half, or whatever," Lorraine replied like it was nothing, texting all the while. Johnson looked at Emily.

"I'll talk to my parents," she said, smiling. Emily tried her best to not to let it get her down, but knowing it was never gonna happen made it hard. Sasha strayed away from the conversation her friends were having about the Hamptons, the celebrities they could see, and the parties they would have. Sasha looked at Talan, who was with Faiday and Ashton, and she couldn't help but feel a little guilty. She didn't know why, because a group of girls were surrounding the boys, and they appeared to be enjoying themselves in the company of them. Talan soon looked at Sasha, and their eyes met for a short time. Talan's eyes almost yearned for approval. Sasha smiled and nodded, signaling it was okay if he was ready to move on. Talan smiled back and started talking to the girls. Sasha knew she was lying to herself if she said that every single time Talan talked to a girl she wouldn't care.

Lily walked right past Talan, while he and his friends talked. Usually, she would lose consciousness just over his existence, but now she didn't care. She walked up to Cliff's locker and opened it. By chance, he was busy with some of his friends and hadn't cleaned out it out yet. She almost wanted to tell him to hurry and do it, because at the end of the day there wouldn't be enough time, but she had other things she wanted to tell him. She left the note on top of his books and closed the locker just she as she heard him say 'bye to some of his friends down the hall. She quickly shut the locker and hid behind a corner as he arrived at his locker and opened it, ready to clean it out. He soon found the note and opened it. Knowing he had received it, she went to the office and asked if she could go home early, since she felt sick. She really did, her heart ached so bad.

Once the last day of freshman year had come to an end, Sasha arrived home, and what met her with anticipation was her mother.

"Mom!" Sasha rushed to her mom and hugged her.

"Sasha?" Lenny asked, confused. Her daughter hadn't shown this much affection toward her in years.

"I missed you so much," Sasha professed.

"I did too, Sasha, but oh, my God, there is nothing better than hot guys and yachts. I wish you could have come; we would have had so much fun." Jeez, Sasha's mom was certifiably insane, wanting to bring her fifteen-year-old daughter to a yacht party.

"Mom, I have to talk to you," Sasha said, breaking down. Lenny almost panicked seeing her daughter cry. She didn't know what to do, so she started with the basics.

"Honey, what's wrong? You're crying," Lenny said, stating the obvious. Sasha grabbed her mother's hand and sat her down on the glass staircase.

"Dad didn't treat me very well," she started. Lenny focused in on what her daughter had to say, and was inescapably trapped in her words. "He did things to me when you weren't around." Lenny grabbed her daughter's hands tighter as Sasha started to explain everything. Lenny, for once, in a very long time, started to cry in front of her daughter.

Emily Parker was in her room contemplating on whether to tell her friend the truth about her family's financial difficulties. She finally summoned up the guts and called Johnson, knowing she couldn't hide the truth forever.

"Hey, I hope you have tons of bathing suits, because the South Hampton beach is amazing," he greeted her. "I'm looking at pictures right now."

"Johnson, I'm sorry, but I don't think I will be able to go."

"Emily, why?" Johnson nagged genuinely.

"With everything going on in the economy"—Emily was pacing around her room, but stopped, knowing that Johnson wasn't going to know what in the hell she was talking about with the economy and such—"I can't afford my share. $40,000 is too much," she admitted.

"Emily—"

"Johnson, my dad had a lot of cutbacks on his salary—"

"No, Emily, listen," Johnson interrupted, "if it's a problem, I can pay for your share."

"Really? No, Johnson, it's way too much. You paid for Hawaii, and the shopping trips."

"Listen, Emily, you're one of my best friends, and if you leave me to go with Lorraine by myself, I swear to God, one of us isn't coming back alive," he said, laughing.

"Okay." Emily smiled. As Emily listened to Johnson, she discovered she didn't need money or boys this early in her life to be happy. She just needed her friends and family . . . and maybe one or two Gucci bags, and some Prada shoes. She quickly jumped into a conversation with Johnson about all the things they could do at the Hamptons.

Back at Johnson's house after he got done talking to Emily, Johnson took three Prozac pills to calm his nerves. He got on his cell and called his therapist—one of the many he was using to manipulate for his need of Prozac.

"Dr. Banks, it's me, Johnson. I'm going to be in the Hamptons this summer, and I needed a refill . . . Okay, thanks. They are really helping me out. I feel so much better . . . No, I haven't been having suicidal thoughts lately. Thanks. Have a nice summer." Johnson hung up, knowing he was going to be taken care of over the summer. Johnson's phone soon started to ring, and it was a call from Julie Kimp, who had been trying to contact Johnson in the last couple of weeks. He smirked and ignored the call, and then discovered he had a text from Talan.

How's Sasha doing?

Talan was waiting for Johnson to text back at his condo. He was hosting a little poolside party. (Well, he really didn't intend for it to happen, but Faiday and Ashton invited all the guests.)

Yeah, she's doing good. Her mom came home today. So we'll c how it goes. Keep an eye on her while we're gone. K

Talan quickly replied.

Yeah, I will without a doubt

Talan walked out to the balcony to join his friends.

"Where were you?" Faiday asked as he entertained one of the girls there.

"Just . . . making a call," Talan answered as he held up his phone.

"Calling your girlfriend?" one of the girls flirtatiously asked.

"Don't have one anymore," he replied.

"Good for me," she said, smiling. Talan smirked, liking the way the girl looked, and dove into the pool.

Chapter Nineteen

Closing

Well, guess this is farewell for three months. We, of course, will still be reporting, but like everybody else we need a break! What will happen to the Hamilton Prep sophomores this summer? Will Lenny and Sasha become closer—like how mothers and daughters are meant to be? Whenever Sasha has a problem, will she ask her mother for advice instead of manipulating the situation and hurting people, and ultimately herself? As Lily flies to DC, will she learn to live and be happy for three months without Cliff? Will Johnson learn how to exist without abusing meds? Will Talan let his walls down again when it comes to love? Will he take his post-Sasha relationships seriously, or will he just revert to his old ways? More importantly, once the new school year begins, will the new freshman class bring on the drama like their predecessors? They have huge stilettos to fill. This is *Miami Teen Social*. Have a wonderful summer . . .

About the Author

Alex Gonzalez began writing in elementary school, where he fell in love with creating new scenes and characters from his imagination. He has written several short stories and young adult novels, but *Wild Prep: Crazy Beautiful Life* is his first published piece. He wrote *Wild Prep* during his sophomore year in high school. As he grew up in a small rural town, Alex's experiences were drastically different than those in *Wild Prep*; however, some teenage experiences are universal. Alex draws upon his own thoughts and feelings to create characters that are believable. He currently lives with his mom and younger brother in Colorado, where he attends school and is in the top ten of his class. He also holds a part-time job, and spends every spare minute he has writing.

About the Book

Talan Merrick is doing whom?
Johnson Sinclair is doing what?
Lily Carrington has a BF, when?
Sasha Chandler got blonder, where?
How do we all know this?
Miami Teen Social . . .

Soft kisses from the sun, mesmerizing, white sandy beaches, a sparkling ocean, mansions, designer clothes—the lives of Miami's young socials are filled with all of these, and especially these—beautiful betrayals, hot addictions, ugly truths, and broken hearts. These kids have it all, and they want more.

Hóla, and bienvenidos to *Miami Teen Social*, a land where the repulsive truth is always lurking behind wholesome perfection.